DEEP COVER

UNDERCOVER – BOOK 1

By Deborah Ballard

DISCLAIMERS:

Although this project is based on a great deal of personal experience and research, this work is fictitious, and any similarities to any persons, alive or dead, are purely coincidental. I mention persons in public life only for purposes of realism, and for that reason alone. I took certain license regarding medical procedures, terms and conditions, and the author is not the fount of all knowledge.

The author accepts the right of the individual to hold his/her/their own political, religious, and social views. There is no intention to offend anyone. If you wish to take offense, that is your choice, but it is not my intent.

PREFACE: THE LGBT EXPERIENCE

This is NOT a cheerful story of a transgender girl who magically transforms into a girl or who has acceptance of family and friends as she transitions. Quite the opposite, this is the story of a transgender girl forced to live as a boy in an environment that is violently opposed to "sissy" boys, "queers", or anyone who is LGBT. The story starts in the 1960s, when they covered up gender ambiguity surgically and repressed as much as possible.

This is a story that attempts to relate, in very real terms, what it is like to be Lesbian, Gay, Bisexual, or Transgender in culture dominated by white Anglo-Saxon Protestants and Catholics who believe that boys must be boys, girls must be girls, and boys must only fall in love with girls, and girls must only fall in love with boys.

This is not a book about transition, which will come later in the series. This book is more focused on the experience of being a transgender girl, knowing you are, and having to pretend you are a boy.

Even though I wasn't aware of it, I wasn't like the other boys. I didn't fight back or push back. In the book, I will share things my parents discovered as they tried to deal with my condition.

I ask the reader to join me in this adventure not as a casual spectator watching something happen to a stranger, but to imagine it was your son, daughter, or grandchild, a niece, nephew, or even a brother.

Table of Contents

Disclaimers: 2

Preface: the LGBT experience 3

Deep Cover 9

Kick a Boy When He's Down 10

New Student - Loving School 12

    WALT 14

    Class...15

    Woody 16

    The First Bully 17

    Asthma 21

New School, New Girl Buddies. 28

    Sissy...29

    Barbies...33

    Trading Clothes 35

    Banished...42

    Self-Taught...52

    Dressing 61

    Cooking..62

    Grandma's Cellar..64

    Cousins 66

Second Grade 69

    GYM...75

Caught in the Act 81

Conversion Therapy 86

Evasion 90

Parent Teacher Conference................................94

Emergency Rooms..99

Hospitalization 103

Lunacy 108

Kennedy..109

Wishes 110

Skin Pops 112

Third Grade..117

Cub Scouts..118

Softball 119

Fourth Grade 122

4H and Hobbies..127

Chemistry and Science.....................................128

Magic and Prayer 129

CARIH—Asthma Study 129

A Breakthrough?..130

Retarded? 132

Gender...138

Spock...139

Spinal Snap 141

Sex Education—Sort of.......................................144

Gay?...145

Teen Idols..147

The Revelation 148

Periods? 152

Shopping 153

Saved 157

Death's Door 159

Almost Over...163

Cramps 164

Nuts!...167

Fairy—Middle School / Jr High............................168

Youth Group..173

Clubs 176

First Dance...178

The Music Died...182

Science 183

One of the Girls 186

First Period 190

Hope...194

Friends 196

Banishment...200

The Sentence..204

Drugs - Experimentation 209

You Have to Fight..215

Escape 220

Witness..225

Shorts 231

More About Sex 235

Holy Spirit 240

The Writer 243

All-City Choir..246

First Kiss 250

Sharing..257

A Party for 16 260

Epilepsy—or Detox 263

Rebellion...268

Gay Bait 269

Valium 272

Chameleon...274

Embracing Diversity..................................278

Addiction and Suicide................................282

Let's put on a Show 283

Summer Theater..289

Getting Pretty 289

Revelation..291

Gina 294

Drama and Theater 296

Assistant Directing....................................298

An Offer You Can't refuse...300

College? 302

Rexxie the Housewife...303

A Leading Role..307

Elder & Priest 308

Gay? 309

Truth 311

Music Man 314

Kit's Cabaret 316

Gay Bar...318

Sherry..320

End Book 1 322

DEEP COVER

This is NOT a cheerful story of a transgender girl who magically transforms into a girl or who has acceptance of family and friends as she transitions. Quite the opposite, this is the story of a transgender girl forced to live as a boy in an environment that is violently opposed to "sissy" boys, "queers", or anyone who is LGBT. The story starts in the 1960s, when they covered up gender ambiguity surgically and repressed as much as possible.

This is a story that attempts to relate, in very real terms, what it is like to be Lesbian, Gay, Bisexual, or Transgender in culture dominated by white Anglo-Saxon Protestants and Catholics who believe that boys must be boys, girls must be girls, and boys must only fall in love with girls, and girls must only fall in love with boys.

This is not a book about transition, which will come later in the series. This book is more focused on the experience of being a transgender girl, knowing you are, and having to pretend you are a boy.

Even though I wasn't aware of it, I wasn't like the other boys. I didn't fight back or push back. In the book, I will share things my parents discovered as they tried to deal with my condition.

I ask the reader to join me in this adventure not as a casual spectator watching something happen to a stranger, but to imagine it was your son, daughter, or grandchild, a niece, nephew, or even a brother.

KICK A BOY WHEN HE'S DOWN

Rex ran down the field, trying to be ready in case the soccer ball came his way. He looked for who he would kick it to, someone who would be better able to score. One of his own teammates tripped him.

"You tripped 'cause you run like a girl", Danny was smaller than the other boys, but very much a bully.

In seconds, eighteen other boys were there, kicking him. They were very careful to kick only the areas covered by clothes. Rex had worn long-sleeved shirts to hide the bruises he had received the day before.

Rex curled up into the fetal position to protect the vital organs below his ribs.

"He looks like a little ball. Let's kick him to the goal line!" Jack was the oldest boy, having flunked one grade.

Randy, a boy who struggled with weight, kicked harder than the others. "You wanna be a girl don't ya!? Sissy!"

Cookie, a bully any time, cried out, "You're a bomb a nation".

Jimmy Gobert laughed. "You're a fairy who plays with Barbie Dolls" as he kicked and stomped Rex's ribs.

The boys from both teams continued to kick and punch Rex for another 15 minutes as Danny put the actual ball into the net. When the bell rang, it saved Rex. The boys left for their next class.

It was over! Rex couldn't move. He just lay there, waiting for the cramps in his muscles to relax. He thought to himself, "What's so terrible about being a girl? I've always wanted to be a girl!". But he would never say it aloud. Not when anyone could hear.

NEW STUDENT - LOVING SCHOOL

Rex and his mother, Lois, arrived at school early enough so that Rex had time to meet the teacher, see the toys, and realize that it was very much like Sunday School.

"Hello young man, I'm Mrs. Andrews, and I will be your teacher this year. What's your name?"

"Pleased to meet you, ma'am, I'm Rex Clark. I'm looking forward to learning to read and write. I already know my ABCs and Numbers!"

Mrs. Andrews turned to Lois. "If that's true, he's likely to be bored. Still, he needs to go to Kindergarten so he will learn the social skills."

"Rex, why don't you go play with the other children."

A few minutes later, another boy came into the class. As his mother left, he started crying. Rex figured the boy needed a friend. If the boy would play nice, maybe Rex could help the boy feel more at home.

Rex went over to the crying boy. "What's your name?"

The boy cried as he said "George". George wasn't crying as long or as loud.

"There are all kinds of fun toys to play with! Would you like to play with me?"

Rex looked over at the little kitchen set on one side of the room. He wanted to play with that.

George stopped crying and went over to a nice little red truck. Rex went over to the George, and played with the boy, picking out a baby blue car.

The two played as more boys and girls started coming in.

Rex noticed a little girl standing by herself. She was wearing pigtails and a pink jumper with little pink bows in her hair, but she looked sad. Rex decided maybe he could be her friend, too.

"I'm Rex, what's your name?"

"I'm Holly."

Rex smiled and said "That's' a pretty name for a pretty girl"

Holly giggled.

"Would you like to play with me?".

Rex smiled a big smile and nodded. "I'd love to play with you. Let's play house! Do you want to take care of the babies or cook dinner?"

Holly went over to the kitchen and Rex followed. They pretended they were cooking and made a pretend dinner.

Holly saw some cute little baby dolls and picked one up.
Rex picked up another doll and cuddled it. He started
singing a lullaby.

Rex started singing "Hush little baby, don't say a word".
He sang softly, like he did when he held his baby
brother. Rex enjoyed taking care of Walt, especially
when he was a baby.

WALT

Rex thought back to that first week after Walt came
home and remembered how he pouted when mom started
saying "Happy Walter's day". Rex even whimpered a
little. His mom asked, "What's wrong, honey?"

Rex said, "It's not fair he just came home and now it's
Walter's day again!".

Both his mom and dad started laughing. His mom said,
"We weren't saying happy Walter's day, we were saying
'Happy Father's Day' to daddy!"

Rex smiled and lifted his shirt.

Lois was puzzled. "What are you doing?".

"I want Walt to eat me too!".

Rex didn't understand why his parents were laughing so hard, but smiled because they did.

"You can't feed him right now, but you can hold him! Would you like that?"

Rex gave a big smile, nodded, and said, "Yes Please!".

He climbed into bed between his mother and father. They put baby Walt into his arms, showing him how to support the little head.

Rex began caressing his cute little hand and feet and started singing a lullaby he had learned from his parents. Soon, Walt seemed to smile.

Here in kindergarten, Rex remembered feeding Walt a bottle. He remembered helping his mother change his diapers. Rex was always so gentle, so patient, and so nurturing. More like the other girls than the boys.

CLASS

The teacher had everyone sit in a circle and asked each of her students to give their name and say something about themselves. She wrote their names on little cards, folded them so that they looked like little tents.

"Each of you has a name tag in front of you. I want you each to copy your name onto the piece of paper in front of you."

Rex had been learning letters from his best friend Meg. She was two years older. He could write his name correctly.

Mrs. Andrews clapped in delight. "Congratulations Rex, you did it right the first time! Do you know the letters?"

"R sounds like Roar, E sounds like echo, X sounds like X-ray."

This stunned Mrs. Andrews. The little boy held secrets.

To Rex, this was very much like Sunday School or bible day camp. Rex loved going to church. He had several friends at the church, some from when they were all babies, and shared a crib.

At church, the teacher would read them bible stories and they would answer questions. They would sing songs like "Jesus Loves Me", and they would memorize Bible verses.

WOODY

The teacher had everyone sit in a circle and asked each of her students to give their name and say something about themselves. She wrote their names on little cards, folded them so that they looked like little tents.

"Each of you has a name tag in front of you. I want you each to copy your name onto the piece of paper in front of you."

Rex had been learning letters from his best friend Meg. She was two years older. He could write his name correctly.

Mrs. Andrews clapped in delight. "Congratulations Rex, you did it right the first time! Do you know the letters?"

"R sounds like Roar, E sounds like echo, X sounds like X-ray."

This stunned Mrs. Andrews. The little boy held secrets.

To Rex, this was very much like Sunday School or bible day camp. Rex loved going to church. He had several friends at the church, some from when they were all babies, and shared a crib.

At church, the teacher would read them bible stories and they would answer questions. They would sing songs like "Jesus Loves Me", and they would memorize Bible verses.

After the brief lesson, the teacher let the kids play a little more. George asked Rex to play with him again, and Rex went over. They started playing with the truck and car again.

Another boy named Greg came over and took the car away from Rex. Rex saw that there were other cars to play with, so he started playing with another one. Greg took that car, too. Several times, Rex would pick up a toy, and the other boy would take it from him.

Rex said, "you have to share!"

The boy was defiant. "No, I don't!" and pushed Rex over.

Rex had been sitting with his legs crossed in a lotus position. He just rolled over backwards. Rex stood up and moved. Soon, several of the boys started pushing him around.

Rex found himself in the room's corner. Boys surrounded him and pushed him. They seemed to want to push him out of existence. The teacher watched, doing nothing, until one boy started hitting Rex. Then others started hitting him.

At that point, the teacher stepped in and told the boys to sit down.

Rex pleaded. "May I play with the girls?"

The teacher gave a worried look and nodded.

The rest of the day went without incident. After lessons in counting and shapes, the class left. Rex's mom, Lois, arrived to pick him up.

Mrs. Andrews went over to a quiet spot where no one would hear.

"Is there a reason that Rex plays so well with the girls?"

Lois nodded. "Rex has been playing with girls since he was about 2. The boys down the street played too rough and kept taking his toys. I was glad when he made friends with the little girl next door."

The teacher had an Aha moment.

"That explains a lot! Rex is so nice that the other boys seem to take advantage. He doesn't posture like the other boys do. Just to be sure, it won't be a problem if he plays with the girls?".

Lois nodded and laughed. "No, not a problem at all. He'll be much happier! It's much safer too. He plays with girls most of the time."

Rex loved school! He learned fast and liked to help the other students learn, too. He was polite, nice, and quiet. Sometimes Rex would have asthma attacks and would have to take medicine. He didn't want to go home. All year long, Rex seemed to prefer playing with the girls. The boys just decided that Rex was nice and stopped trying to push him around and take his things.

In first grade, as the lessons got harder and longer. Rex seemed to love to learn. He loved to read aloud when it was his turn and made few mistakes. Sometimes he would even read ahead to see how the story would go. Unlike most of the boys, Rex didn't laugh when someone made a mistake. Instead, gave a friendly smile, to help the reader get over their fear.

One day, his friend Holly came to school wearing a pair of shiny black tights. Rex sat next to her in reading.

"Those tights are pretty and shiny. Do they feel nice?"

Holly nodded and grabbed Rex's hand and put it on her leg so he could feel them.

"They feel nice! I got them last night."

It was like his satin comforter that his grandmother made for him.

The teacher intervened.

"Let's get back to the lesson, Rex. Can you read next?"
Life went on as normal.

One day, during recess, Rex's friend Veronica showed
Rex how to swing up and climb into the hub of the rings.
It seemed very high, but they loved being up there and
with each other.

Sometimes, if the boys had been mean, Rex and
Veronica would pull up all the rings. That was when the
teacher would step in to discourage such behavior.

"Vera, you need to let the other kids have their turns.
You and Rex need to come down now."

That winter, the boys played King of the Hill on a high
snowdrift, but each time Rex tried to climb, the other
boys would push him down with their feet. He made it to
the top for a few seconds before someone knocked him
down. Still, Rex had fun and giggled as he watched other
boys being pushed down.

One of his friends from church, Allen, was in second
grade. Even though he was only a month older than Rex,
Allen got the respect of being a year "older". Sometimes,
Alan would protect Rex from the rougher boys.

Rex was having health problems. He had to be hospitalized 3 times that year, once right after Thanksgiving and once after Christmas. Each time he went to the hospital, they would try to stick an IV needle in his arm, but the veins would roll, and they would have to try again, the first time they had to stick him almost 30 times. They put it into his foot, then taped his foot to a board. It was excruciating! Rex found it very hard to sleep.

Rex couldn't figure out why they were hurting him so much. He must have done something terrible because this hurt MUCH worse than a spanking.

He kept crying out. "I'll be good, please don't hurt me again."

Since his mom and dad seemed as upset as he was, Rex decided maybe God was punishing him for something. It must have been horrible. There was so much pain! He just wanted to die.

For the first week in the hospital, Rex would be in an oxygen tent, with no television, no radio, and nothing that could cause sparks or fire. In addition, the medications included drugs that would keep him wide awake most of the day and night. Often Rex would only get 2-3 hours of fitful sleep and even then, only in brief spurts. The biggest challenge was fighting the boredom.

Lois realized Rex got very bored in the hospital, so she taught him how to crochet and gave him some acrylic yarn. Rex started by making a potholder, then a hat, and then larger items. She also found "brain teaser" games for him to play.

Tom brought some books about science. He bought books on chemistry and brought in magazines like Popular Science and Popular Mechanics. They were far above Rex's reading level. Rex had lots of time on his hands. He could read the stories. He understood most of the articles.

During the second hospitalization, the doctor pulled Rex's parents aside. "We found mold in his nasal passages and his tonsils need to come out".

Tom shook his head. "Are you saying we need to move?"

The doctor told him, "Yes, move as soon as possible, otherwise the asthma will get worse. Here is a list of things to look for to help you find a safe home."

"Forced air heat? Electrostatic air cleaner? No wallpaper? No mold? Newer than 10 years old? Doc, a house like that will cost us a fortune!"

"Would you rather pay a fortune in hospital and medical bills?"

Tom and Lois went to dinner with Rex while Meg's parents watched Walt.

"Tom, you've been talking about moving to the suburbs for months now, so what's the problem?"

"When that black family moved in at the end of the block, I thought everybody would panic sell. We could lose all our equity. Instead, it seems like everybody is OK with it."

"I'm upset that you could even THINK about being racist! Rex loves playing with their daughter, and her mother loves to have coffee with us. We often go to her house. Her house is cleaner than mine. I'm impressed with the whole family. Did you know her husband was a lawyer?"

"You have a point there. I have seen Rex playing with the little girl. She's polite. I only know the neighbors from church. They are a wonderful family. They even took care of Rex when you were at Mount Airy."

"So why don't you want to move?"

"I don't like being told that I HAVE to move! My doctor told me I HAD to move to the Southwest for my asthma. I thought it would go away, but I still get asthma. I had a full scholarship at Cornel, but I had to go to Arizona. The doctor didn't guarantee that this new house would fix either of us."

"I think Bruce & Julie's house has many of those features. She might give us the name of a good realtor who could find us a suitable house."

The next day, Lois went to Julie's house.

"Tom and I have to look for a house in the suburbs, and we have all these special requirements. Do you like it here in Virginia Village?"

"It's nice. The houses are smaller than yours. Most don't have basements. They built them on pads with crawl spaces and a shallower foundation. There's a house about a block away that's a little bigger. I'll give you the number of our Real Estate agent."

Lois and Tom met with the agent to see the house.

"This house is on a corner lot, which means you get a lot more real estate. There's also a hedge around the front yard so you won't have so many kids just walking through your yard. It also has the forced air heat you wanted, and it has a storm cellar style area instead of a full basement. As a result, you have room for storage, and you can more easily access the furnace."

"Does it have the air cleaner?"

"When you asked about that, I found a contractor. He could put it in for about $300, which you can add to your home mortgage. The sellers will put it in if you increase your offer by $500."

"OK, we'll increase our offer. Lois, this had better fix the problems for both Rex and me. I'm sick of doctors promising that we won't have asthma if we make unreasonable sacrifices. Only to find out we still have asthma."

They showed Rex around the house and showed him what would be the room he shared with Walt.

"So, Rex, what color would you like us to paint it?"

"I'd like you to point it turquoise. A blend of blue and pink."

At the end of March, Rex went to the hospital for the tonsillectomy, while his parents moved to the new house. They painted his room turquoise.

One of the more interesting parts was when the Rex woke up on the operating table, as the doctor was putting in some stitches.

The doctor shouted, "He's awake, put him out quick!"

During the operation, Rex had several nightmares about being in a swimming pool with a bunch of sharks. The recovery was OK. At least he got to eat lots of ice cream. He couldn't swallow anything else. The ice cream helped his sore throat feel better, too.

The night after the operation, the nurse had to give him a shot to help him sleep.

"I don't want a shot! They hurt so much! Can't I take a pill instead?"

The nurse understood. "Your throat is too sore for pills and we don't want to make that worse. I'll tell you what. I'll show you how to relax your muscles so that the needles won't hurt so much. Would that be OK?"

Rex rolled onto his tummy. The nurse massaged his gluteus maximus until she could feel that no tension. Then she inserted the needle and slowly injected the serum.

"That wasn't so bad, was it?"

Rex shook his head. "No, that didn't hurt at all! I need to do that every time. Can I do the same thing with my arm?"

"Yes, it works with your arms, too. It can even help with IVs.

NEW SCHOOL, NEW GIRL BUDDIES.

Rex started at the new school the Monday after he got out of the hospital. He liked new teacher.

"Hello Rex, my name is Miss Cody. Pleased to meet you."

"You mean like Buffalo Bill Cody?!"

"Yes! Buffalo Bill was my great uncle. I'm surprised you know about him!"

"My grandmother grew up in Missouri and Colorado. Buffalo Bill's grave is up in the mountains. It's on the way to a cabin we rented this summer."

"Why don't you sit down here and we'll start with reading."

When it was Rex's turn to read, he read with no hesitations. His advanced skills startled Miss Cody.

"My friend Meg taught me had to read, so I read to her every day. I read aloud to my mom too."

He also knew his numbers and could write short sentences. He also did well with math, but that was harder.

At recess, the boys started going down the slide.

"Rex, climb up and slide down, but watch out, the girls will try to kiss you and give you Cooties!"

The boy went first. When he got to the bottom, he looked like he was being tortured and was hating it.

"Oh yucky! Cooties!! Get off!! Make them stop!!"

SISSY

When it was Rex's turn, he went down the slide. He relaxed, like he did with the shots. The girls started kissing him and he just laid there and let them kiss him.

Then he got up he said, "That was fun! The boys think that is terrible. I don't know why. It's like kissing my mom and getting kissed. I like this kissing too!"

One girl asked, "Rex, would you like to play jump rope?"

"You only use one rope? At my old school we used two. Otherwise only one of us would get a turn."

Rex could skip for about 20 turns and missed. Someone else could take a turn. He held the rope so that the other girls could take their turns. There were new rhymes, but Rex learned them in a few minutes.

"That was fun! I enjoy playing with you girls!"

The boys got upset. This new boy was strange.

Stevie shouted, "Rex, what are you, a SISSY!"

"Yeah, he's a SISSY freak!" Jimmy shoved him.

"Yeah, a SISSY who wants to be a GIRL!"

Johnny pushed him down and kicked him.

The bell range signaling the end of recess.

Miss Cody addressed the threats against Rex.

"Class, I heard some of you calling someone a Sissy. Does anybody know what a Sissy is?"

"Yeah, it's a stupid boy who wants to play with GIRLS! Yuck!" Jimmy got a big laugh from the boys.

"Very good Jimmy. That's not quite right. A Sissy is a boy who is friends with girls. How many of you boys call Jan a Buddy?"

"We ALL do! Jan is great. She's as tough as any of us boys, and she doesn't mind getting dirty. She's fun to play with."

"Well, Johnny, 'Buddy' is a slang name for Brother. So when you call Jan a Buddy, you are making her an honorary brother. It's a high honor."

Jan flexed her muscles. "Yeah! I love being your Buddy! Thank you guys!"

Miss. Cody continued. "So if a boy is a Sissy, the girls have accepted him as a Sister, that is also a high honor."

Cathy chirped, "Yeah, we like Rex! He's like one of us girls! We're glad he is our friend."

Rex held his head high. "Yes, and I am proud to have such wonderful friends as Cathy, Karen, Sally, Missy, and the rest of the girls. They are smart and fun!"

Miss. Cody drove the point home. "So, you boys should stop calling anyone a SISSY like it was some terrible thing! It's like telling people your moms are terrible, or that I'm terrible, or that any other woman you love is a terrible person. Understand!"

Cathy, the blonde with curly hair, replied. "We like playing with you too, Rex. Do you ride the bus?"

"I will, but my mom is picking me up today. She wanted to talk to Miss. Cody."

The teacher watched with great curiosity. Rex not only didn't mind playing with girls, but he also enjoyed playing with them.

Lois picked Rex up. The office sent to Miss. Cody's room.

"Hi Rex, how was your first day at this new school?"

"It was great, mom! I made a bunch of new friends. Cathy, Karen, and Sally live on the same street as us!"

"That's great honey, I need to talk to you teacher for a few minutes. Can you just sit in the back and color?"

"I it's a pleasure to meet you Mrs. Clark! Rex is a remarkable boy! He reads exceptionally well, he is polite and respectful, and he has excellent social skills. He's become popular with most of the girls!"

"Call me Lois. I'm glad he's getting along. He has played with girls most of his life. He has asthma and gets dangerous attacks when he plays with the boys. They play too rough. He will have medications with him. He can take them if he has an attack."

"That explains many things. It quite surprised me when Rex just started playing with the girls. He was jumping rope, but I realized he missed the jump so the other girls could have a turn."

"He's pretty good about sharing and taking turns. Something he learned from his best friend meg. She's two years older than he is. They've been friends since he could talk."

"So I assume it won't be a problem if he plays with the girls here at school."

"No, of course not! It's probably best for everybody."

BARBIES

A few days later, Rex rode the school bus to school and back home. Several girls that got off at his stop.

Cathy, a girl with curly blond hair, asked; "Rex, would you like to play Barbie's with us at my house?"

Rex thought they said babies. "Yes, that sounds like a lot of fun."

He went with the girls to Cathy's house, where she had several Barbie dolls. She handed one to Rex.

"This doll looks like a grownup! Didn't you want to play with baby dolls?"

"No, we dress the Barbies in different outfits. Then we trade clothes!"

"Oh, that sounds like fun, too. Can I pick some out?"

"Yes, let's see what you think looks pretty."

Rex looked at the clothes scattered on the floor.

"That white skirt looks pretty. I'll try a blue blouse and the black boots. She'll look a bit like Jackie Kennedy."

Rex spent about 10 minutes dressing the doll and getting everything to look just right.

Karen, a brunette, gawked. "Wow Rex, you're right, she looks like Jackie. You have great taste! Pick out another one."

They continued to play for about two hours until Cathy's mother came home.

"Hi mom! Karen, Sheryl and I invited Rex over to play Barbie."

"Ok Cathy, don't be silly! Boys don't want to play with Barbie dolls, you shouldn't tease him like that!"

"It's OK ma'am, I've never played with Barbie dolls before. I have played with baby dolls. At home, I treat my stuffed animals like they were babies. Barbie dolls are fun too!"

"Rex has great taste, mom! He's put together 5 outfits that look wonderful together! One looked like Jackie Kennedy, another looked like Nancy Sinatra. Another one looked like Annette Funicello!"

Rex played with several of the girls after school, and before long, he friends with all of them.

Cathy's mother, Muriel, accepted Rex as 'one of the girls'.

TRADING CLOTHES

One day, Cathy asked, "Hey, why don't we trade clothes?".

Karen, a girl with long wavy brown hair, asked. "What about Rex? We can't leave Rex out!"

Cathy said, "I have a pretty dress Rex can wear. It will be his official entry into the 'Girls Club'".

Karen wanted to wear Rex's clothes.

"Rex, please let me try on your jeans and your flannel shirt! I've always wanted to dress like a boy!"

Rex took off his shirt. "OK. Here, it's sorta clean. Mom washed it and I've only worn it today. Cathy, do you have some shorts or a skirt I can wear? I'm a little bashful."

Cathy pulled out a package of underwear from her drawer, a skirt, and a blouse. "You can wear the skirt, but you have to change into some clean underwear. Mom told me that boy's underwear is dirty. I don't want you messing up my clothes."

Rex went into the bathroom and changed into the underwear and the skirt. Then he put on the blouse.

"How do I look?"

Cathy shook her head. "You still look too much like a boy. I have just the thing."

Karen tried on Rex's jeans and frowned.

"How can you wear these? It's like wearing sandpaper, and they look terrible!".

She tried on the flannel shirt.

"This shirt itches bad. I think I'm getting a rash!"

Cathy came out with a teal blue dress with balloon sleeves and a high collar.

"Rex, try this on. It should look pretty on you."

Cathy helped Rex into the dress.

Rex smiled. "How do I look?"

Cheryl, a girl with short auburn hair, squealed in delight. "Rex, you look so pretty. Too bad your hair's so short or you'd be a pretty girl!".

"That looks much better! You look pretty now! Put these tights on. They will make you look even more like a girl."

Rex hesitated.

"Sit on the bed and I'll help you put them on."

Rex had watched her mother put on stockings. Cathy gathered up one leg and pulled it up Rex's leg, just past his knee.

"Let me try the other leg."

Rex pulled up the other leg, and after a few adjustments, the tights were all the way up.

Once dressed, Rex had an almost blissful smile on his face. It was like the goosebumps he got when his mother would caress his back or hold him. There was a calm. It was like when he was being held by his parents or grandparents, or when he was helping someone. It just felt Right.

"I like this! It's pretty! It feels nice. I wish my hair wasn't so short. All three of you have such pretty hair. I look stupid with my fuzzy hair. I hate it when my grandpa cuts my hair. He shaves it so close it hurts. I just want to grow it out!"

"Oh Rex, you're so pretty! We love having you as our new friend. You look pretty in my dress!"

Karen was still in Rex's clothes. "We like you Rex. This started out as a joke, but you've been so nice about it. We love having you as our friend."

Rex felt at home, loved, and happy. "I like you guys too. You are wonderful friends. I'm glad I get to play with you."

Since Karen was wearing Rex's clothes, Rex had to stay in Cathy's dress. Before long, Rex liked the dress more than he his boy clothes.

The girls, including Rex, continued to play together. They played Jacks and Go Fish and played Barbies together. When Cathy's mother came home, Cathy couldn't wait to introduce her new friend.

"Mom, come and see Rexy, she's so pretty!"

When Cathy's mom, Muriel, walked into the room, she looked like she'd seen something horrible. She started screaming.

"Rex, what the hell do you think you're doing! You're EVIL, You're an ABOMINATION! You are going to end up in HELL! Get out of those clothes and put on your clothes and go home right now. I'm calling your mother to tell her what a horrible thing you've done!"

Rex was so confused he didn't know what to say. Karen changed into her skirt and blouse so Rex could have his clothes back. Rex went into the bathroom to change.

When he came out, Muriel grabbed him by the ear and dragged him out the door as he cried. She pushed him out the door and screamed. "Don't you EVER come here again!".

Muriel was so furious! She called Miss Cody.

"You wouldn't believe what I saw in my daughter's room this evening! It was terrible! Rex was sitting there playing JACKS with my daughter and her friends. He was wearing one of my daughter's dresses! I couldn't believe it!"

"Yes, most girls that age play jacks."

"He must be a little pervert! An abomination, I tell you! He's evil! We need to do everything we can to keep him away from the other girls!"

Miss Cody rushed to Rex's defense. "I've talked to his mother. Rex doesn't play well with the boys. He doesn't fight back or rough house, so all the other boys take advantage of him. Sometimes it even gets violent.".

Muriel snapped back. "I think you should FORCE him to play with the other boys! It will do him some good. Maybe if he weren't such a SISSY, he could play with the other boys. He would stop molesting our daughters!"

The teacher softened. "Rex was hospitalized several times this year. I don't know if he can take the stress of playing with the boys if things go bad."

Muriel made it clear. "Listen here Miss Cody, you either keep that pervert away from our daughters. Or I will have the principal start the process for your dismissal. I've already talked to him. He understands my feelings. He even told me he would have Rex expelled if he didn't stop playing with the girls!"

Cody couldn't believe what she was hearing. Rex was such a sweet little boy. He did nothing inappropriate with the girls. In fact, the girls seemed to have a great deal of fun molesting him. And unlike the other boys, he didn't seem to mind. Rex was so nice and polite. She knew things would not go well if she forced Rex to play with the boys.

The next morning, Cody came to school early to do her lesson prep. Principal Harris was there just a few minutes after she came in. Principal Harris looked like somebody had just died or was about to.

"Did you get a call from Muriel last night?"

"Yes, I did. She seemed quite upset! Something about Rex wearing a dress!".

Harris sighed; "You don't know the half of it! Muriel called all her friends at church. They called all the parents of the first graders in the PTA. One of whom contacted the school board. Someone even called the mayor. It wouldn't surprise me if the Governor got a call."

I was fielding calls all night long from parents who wanted Rex expelled, arrested, or worse. Some even threatened to harm him. It wasn't just the girls' parents, either. Even the boys' parents were calling.

This could get ugly. Some the parents got some strange stories. Some thought Rex molested one girl. Others thought he raped all the girls. Gossip can get so ugly.

Cody couldn't believe her ears. "I hate sending him out to play with the boys. They are already violent to him. I'm afraid that some of those boys might do something dangerous!"

Harris stiffened. "This isn't one of those inner-city schools where they might allow such things. These parents are rich, powerful, and influential. Several have friends on the Board of Education, as well as the city and state legislatures. They could make life hell for us if we don't do what they ask."

That same morning, Rex got on the bus.

"You can't sit with us, Rex. Sit with the BOYS!"

Rex moved further back.

"Go away SISSY. Sit with the GIRLS!"

Rex turned back to the girls, only to see rows of scowling faces.

He whispered. "I guess I'm all alone now."

He walked to the very back of the bus. He found a seat by himself.

BANISHED

The day went fine until recess. Cody dreaded what was about to come. She knew it wouldn't be pretty.

"I'm sorry Rex, you can't play with the girls today. You've got to go out onto the grass and play with the boys. I'm sure that they will play some fun games."

Cody thought to herself, "Fun for them, but not for Rex." She hung her head in shame.

Rex tried to be his cheerful self. Was he naïve or stupid? Was he just being too hopeful?

"OK Miss. Cody. I'll go play with the boys. They were nice to me on my first day. I'll try to play the games they play. I just have to learn how."

Rex came over to the group of boys playing in the grass.

"Hi guys, can I play with you today?"

Jimmy called out. "We're playing war, pull up a clod of grass and throw it at the boys on the other side, and try not to get hit."

Rex threw a few tiny dirt clods, but they didn't go very far.

"Can't you throw any better than that?"

"You're not even close!"

"My baby sister could throw better than you."

"You throw like a girl!"

"You're a stupid SISSY!"

One boy on the other side threw a rock at Rex and hit him in the forehead.

"That's how you're supposed to throw!"

Rex cried. "You threw a ROCK! That's against the RULES!"

Boys on his own side started throwing rocks at him.

"Yeah!?! This is WAR, there are no RULES!"

Soon, all 16 of the boys were throwing rocks at Rex. At first he tried to dodge them, but soon the tears blurred his vision and he couldn't see them coming.

They chanted, "STONE THE SISSY!"

Others shouted, "KILL THE FAGGOT".

They surrounded and terrified Rex. He screamed for help. He could see the teacher, but she didn't make a move to help him. Soon, more rocks were drawing blood. One rock hit Rex just below the eye.

"Oh my God! Rex is bleeding!"

Rex ran toward Miss. Cody. He was crying, his hand over his right eye. There was blood on his right hand.

Miss. Cody felt panic rising.

"Let me see Rex. Pull you hand away from your eye. Thank goodness that rock didn't hit your eye. Your cheek is bleeding. I'll have someone take you to the nurse."

She blew her whistle. "ALL RIGHT! RECESS is OVER NOW! Everybody back to class NOW!"

She turned to Karen, who had been one of Rex's friends.

"Karen, could you walk Rex to the Nurse's Office? Come straight back!"

"Yes, Miss. Cody. Come on Rex, follow me. Here's a Kleenex for your eye."

Karen's mother had not told her not to play with Rex. In fact, it disgusted her when she got the call after midnight from a woman she knew from the PTA, a woman she disliked. The woman knew nothing about Rex and her claims were preposterous.

Karen had told her mom about putting Rex in a dress, and her wearing Rex's clothes. She got a laugh when Karen told her how much Rex's clothes scratched and itched.

Karen got Rex to the nurse. She had to hold his left hand because he couldn't see. When they got to the nurse's office, Karen wanted to help.

"Rex and the boys were throwing rocks on the playground and Rex got hurt."

Rex fought the tears. "I wasn't throwing rocks, only clods. Then ALL THE boys started throwing rocks at me!"

Karen went back to class as directed by Miss Cody.

The nurse put a butterfly bandage on the gash and said, "that should hold you until you get home. Maybe you won't need stitches."

The scar would remain for life, both on his face and in his memory.

Rex went back to class by himself. He knew where the room was. He wanted to go home, but he would have to wait until the bus took him home.

When Rex returned to class, they were in a circle for reading.

"Oh! Rex! You're back! It's time for reading. Sit between Jimmy and Tommy."

Rex sat down and read silently as the other kids each took their turns. When they got to Rex, Rex started reading.

Jimmy whispered, "Sissy! Wait until after school. You're dead. We might even beat you up on the bus."

Rex tried to keep reading, but lost his place.

Tommy whispered. "We're gonna beat you up before school, too! You're a sissy faggot!"

Rex was on the verge of crying again and couldn't read anymore.

Miss Cody heard the threats. She tried to be comforting, but Rex would have to read aloud tomorrow.

That night, after they got off the bus, Jimmy called out, "Rex, come on over to my house. I've got something to show you."

Rex thought to himself. "Maybe the boys will be nice to me now."

The boy's house was in the opposite direction from Rex's house. After they were about a block away, five boys picked up large sticks about two inches in diameter.

Jimmy laughed. "We won't let you join our club, but we will hit you with OUR clubs!"

Rex ran as fast as he could, but the boys were chasing him away from home. In seconds, five boys were swinging their clubs. They hit Rex in the stomach, back, and legs, so that none of the damage would show.

When it was over, Rex just laid there on the ground, wishing that it would all be over. Every muscle in his body screamed in pain. Even moving his legs to change position was so painful, he just wanted to lie there. He hoped he would pass out or maybe even just die.

Standing was a tremendous effort, and he limped as he walked to his house.

Lois was in the family room at the back of the house and hadn't seen the attack. She had been smoking. A cloud of smoke filled the room.

Rex came in crying. "I hate boys! I wish I was a girl!"

He went into his room to lie down.

At dinner, his parents noticed the butterfly bandage.

"How did you get that?" Tom didn't want to touch it.

"The boys were throwing rocks at me, and one almost hit me in the eye."

"My God! You have cuts and bruises all over your face. How many rocks were there?"

"Too many to dodge."

That night, when Rex was ready for bed, Lois could see the bruises on his arms and legs. She opened his pajama shirt, horrified. There were bruises on almost every inch of his body, from his neck to the elbows and almost to the ankles.

Lois asked, "Who did this to you."

"The boys."

"Which boys,"

"All the boys in my class."

"How many boys were there?"

Rex cried. "About 8 of them, and they all had sticks."

Lois left the room, furious. She was almost yelling at Tom.

"We just moved into this nice new house. This should be a better neighborhood! Now Rex is in more danger than he was at the old school."

Tom tried to calm her.

"Maybe this is just a phase. Boys often pick on the new kid. It's like fraternity hazing."

Lois got tried to calm. "We need to know who we should talk to that would stop these attacks. Do we know any good lawyers?"

The next day, Rex went to school and felt abandoned. Even the girls were making fun of him. The boys continued to make threats throughout the day.

When they had a bathroom break, Rex sat down. The stalls had no doors.

Jimmy jeered, "Oh wow, Rex has to sit to pee, LIKE A GIRL! Let's pull him out, maybe he's a girl pretending to be a boy!"

They terrified Rex. "No, I need to poop! Leave me alone!"

The boys kicked him and hit him. "Come on Rex, let's SEE you so-called poop." They pulled him out of the stall.

When he got up, the boys started laughing even more.

"There's no poop in the bowl, Rex. Only toilet paper!"

Tommy just pointed.

"Look! No wonder he wanted to play with the girls. He sits to pee because he CAN'T pee standing up."

The boys held his arms.

"It's so small! It doesn't look like a penis at all! My baby brother has one twice as big as that! He's only 1-year-old!"

"Does he even have balls? It doesn't look like he has anything down there?"

"I can't believe it. He DOESN'T have balls! He doesn't even have a bag for them!"

"No wonder you're such a SISSY! You don't even have proper boy bits!"

"Maybe we can stretch his little thing out! Maybe it's just stuck inside, like a girl!"

One boy grabbed it and pulled hard. Rex screamed out in pain!

"Miss Cody! HELP! HELP!"

One boy held their hand over his mouth. Another boy punched him hard in the solar plexus.

"Shut up. Nobody likes a tattle-tale."

"Yeah! Stool pigeons get hurt!" followed by another punch to the gut.

"If you tell, we will beat you up even worse!"

Miss Cody had heard Rex screaming, but she couldn't go into the boys' bathroom. It violated school policy. Unfortunately, there were only a few male teachers. None of them were close enough to help.

All the other boys filed out. Rex was the last one out.

"What happened in there, Rex? I heard you scream!"

Rex looked terrified. "Nothing. I'm sorry I screamed."

Miss Cody saw Rex looking terrified at someone behind her. She didn't turn in time to see Jimmy shaking his fist as a threat.

At recess, the boys attacked Rex again. This time, they just tripped him and kicked him. Miss Cody watched in horror as every boy in her class assaulted him. She went over to pull Rex out of the mob.

"I hate this school! I wish I was back at my old school! I wish I was back with my REAL FRIENDS! Holly, Veronica, Theresa, and Mary were my friends. They were NICE to me!"

At school, Rex would hear whispered threats all day long.

When it came time to answer questions, he would answer correctly, but almost like a zombie.

He had no enthusiasm at all. When it was Rex's turn to read aloud, Rex couldn't read because he was trying not to cry.

Reading was just after recess, and he'd get assaulted—every day. The boys would trip him. About 10 of them would start kicking him like they were kicking a ball. They stayed in a tight huddle so that the teacher couldn't see how badly Rex was being hurt.

At night, Rex couldn't sleep at all. He couldn't fall asleep and woke to terrifying nightmares of beatings. He woke up before sunrise. On a good night, he would get 3 hours of total sleep, in fitful naps.

SELF-TAUGHT

Rex withdrew and isolated. It was just after recess.

"Rex, it's your turn to read. This is the third time I've asked, pay attention."

Rex was in so much pain he wanted to throw up. He just started crying. "I can't!"

Miss Cody ran out of patience. She knew he was hurting, but she wanted him to stand up to the bullies by showing he was smart.

"Rex, you must read now. Please continue where we left off."

Rex hadn't slept all week. The daily trauma was causing so much stress, he was about to snap. Worse, he knew the trauma would happen again after school, at bathroom breaks, and at lunch and recess every day until the end of the school year.

Rex had watched Miss Cody stand there and do nothing as the boys were hurting him. Even when he cried out, she did nothing. She was as bad as the boys were. There was anger and defiance in his voice.

"I don't WANT to read!"

Miss Cody couldn't accept this defiance.

"You WILL read, NOW!"

Rex was furious! Now she was trying to humiliate him in front of the entire class.

"I WON'T read. I can read, but I WON'T read aloud!"

"Fine, you can sit on the other side of the room. You can read to the SLOW kids later."

Rex didn't even care anymore. He had already read the entire book to himself. He knew all the words and could have read aloud. At least the slow class didn't have to read right after recess. Also, he didn't have to sit between the two worst bullies, Jimmy and Tommy, who would threaten him throughout reading.

Something caught his attention.

"OK, for those of you on THIS side of the class, we will move on to the next book. It's called 'Dick and Jane Play Ball', it's a reward for all of you who have done so well in your reading class."

Rex raised his hand from the other side of the room.

"Miss Cody, that was the book I was reading at my old school. Can I read that book too?"

Miss Cody knew Rex was more than capable of reading the new book, but she couldn't accept his defiance and wanted him to calm down after recess.

"I'm sure you did, Rex, but since you can't read aloud in this group, stay in YOUR reading group."

Rex wasn't even nice. "This is STUPID! I don't belong in the slow group! I don't belong in this class! I don't even belong in this SCHOOL!"

Rex came home and started crying as he walked through the door. He told his mom about being put on the 'dumb' side, and about the 'smart' kids reading the book he had already read at his old school.

That Saturday, Lois took Rex to the public library and got him a library card.

"This is a library card. You can use it to pick out up to 6 books. Any books you like! You can keep them for up to 3 weeks. Then we come back and give back those books and you can get 3 more."

About 20 minutes later, Rex came back with 4 books. "I found the book I was reading at my old school! I also found three more books about girls!"

Lois loved to see that Rex had attempted to find some books. "Let's see if we can find a book about boys, too. Maybe that will help you get along with the boys at school."

"I tried to find books about boys, but the boys seemed to do yucky things. They only seemed to want to throw things and get into fights. I'll get one if I have to."

He went to get the least annoying of the books.

Rex finished reading "Dick and Jane Play Ball" that afternoon. He then went on to another book about girls. That night, he had finished the book. He looked very sad.

"I liked this book. It reminded me of the things I did with Cathy, Karen, Vicky, and the other girls. I miss them so much!" Rex bawled as he finished. "Why won't they play with me anymore?"

Lois had been to a "Coffee Klatch" with the other wives on the block. Muriel didn't know Lois. She began ranting about Rex in the group.

"That boy, Rex, is a terrible little pervert! He molested my daughter and other girls IN MY HOUSE! He even tricked them into letting him wear my daughter's clothes! It was disgusting. He was wearing her tights, her shoes, her dress, and even her panties."

Karen's mother came to Rex's defense. "Rex has played at our house many times. He's so polite! So friendly! He loves playing with the girls, but he always plays nicely with them!"

Muriel got flustered. "What would you know about it! I came home from work and caught him in the act! I wasn't having any of it! He was out of those clothes in no time. I'd have thrown him out onto the street naked if I didn't think he would parade around naked! He cried as I dragged him out by his ear!"

Lois put down her cup. "If you'll excuse me, I need to get home. Rex will be home in about an hour. He's upset, because he has no friends!"

After she left, Muriel seemed quite pleased with herself. "Well, I guess we won't be inviting HER to any more of these little meetings!"

Vicky's mom seethed. "Haven't you done enough damage at this point, Muriel! I'm not thirsty anymore. Time to get home to greet MY kids. It would be terrible for anyone to spread false RUMORS about them behind my back!"

Adele, who lived next door to Lois and Tom, took Muriel's side. "I, for one, don't want my daughters to have anything to do with Rex. That family is just strange."

Muriel huffed. "I'm surprised you feel that way. Rex's father gives your husband a jump start three times a week. Can't your husband afford a new car battery, Adele?"

Adele gave out as good as she got. "Well, at least I don't have to work at a full-time job. I know what my daughters do because I am there when they get home."

That afternoon, Rex came home from school. Lois had been sitting at the kitchen window and watched as the boys tackled Rex in the yard across the street. She watched in horror as they started kicking him and punching him. Then they ran off down the street.

Rex came in crying. Lois held him close. "I saw those boys beating you up. Why?"

"Because I am a SISSY GIRL! I HATE being a boy. Please let me be a girl instead! Please let me grow my hair out so I can play with the other girls!"

Lois couldn't believe her ears. Her son was hurting, but his request made no sense.

"Why don't you go to your room and read one of your books. Then you can help me make dinner. We can have hamburgers!"

Rex stopped crying. "I've read them all already! They made me sad. The book about boys was stupid! The ones about girls just made me miss my friends. Why won't Miss Cody let me play with the girls?"

Lois knew the answer. It just made her that much more upset at Muriel. "I'm sure she has her reasons. Why don't you want to play with the boys?"

"The boys beat me up! They pull me out of the bathroom stall! I have to take Kao-Pectate so that I won't have to go poop. Even when I stand up, they make fun of me and beat me up. They beat me up at recess and at lunch, then after school when we get off the bus."

Lois did the math. Based on when Rex came home with the bruises, they had already assaulted Rex at least 80 times. There were still 3 weeks before the end of the school year.

That night, Tom came home and Lois had fixed an early dinner.

"Tom, could you take Rex to the library tonight? He's read all the books he checked out from the library and wants to get more."

"Already! Rex, you checked out those other books about a week ago! Have you read them all?"

"Yes, I liked the ones about the girls, but I missed playing with my old friends. The one about boys was yucky."

"I'm impressed. OK! I'll take you to the library tonight. Maybe you can read some non-fiction books!"

"What are non-fiction books?"

"Those are books that describe how things work, or how to do things. You like to help your mom cook. Maybe you can find a book on how to cook! I'll help you pick out some books."

Tom took Rex to the library. They found the children's section. Tom showed Rex a book about cooking. Then he pulled out a book about electricity.

"I work for a company that makes electricity. This book would tell you more about electricity."

Tom opened the book and realized that it might be above his reading level. "Can you read this?"

Rex opened it up and read aloud. "Yes, I think I can work out the hard words. I can ask you or mom for help if I have words I don't know."

Rex looked for more books in the children's section. "I'm going to look for some harder kid's books. The books at school are too easy. I wish Meg could help me. I loved reading her books."

"Wait! Meg is in third grade! Are you telling me you can read her books?"

"Sure! Meg loves teaching me how to read! She loves reading harder books too. She got some of her books from Bruce."

Bruce was in 6th grade. If Rex was reading his books, it was easy to understand why Rex had gone through all 6 of his beginning reader books in a week.

"Let's pick out a couple more together. I'll try to pick some out, and you tell me if they are too hard to read."

They found 4 more books to give Rex 6. Tom got his own library card and checked out some books for himself. As an adult, he could get more books, so he got two more for Rex.

By the end of the summer, Rex was reading at 6th grade level. Karen and Vicky played with him over the summer, but only when Cathy and Cheryl weren't there. It was a lonely summer.

DRESSING

One night, Rex woke up in the middle of the night. Something in the bathroom caught his attention. It looked like a dark shape on the laundry hamper was a monster. He knew it was just a trick of the light, so he got up to check it out.

Lois had left some clothes on top of the hamper because it was full. Rex saw they were the pretty clothes his mother wore to church, Rex tried them on.

Her skirt was way too big, but the slip seemed to fit. The girdle differed from the underwear. It had a pretty and shiny front that reminded him of his favorite blanket. The stockings were much lighter and softer than tights. They felt so nice.

The feelings he had when he played with Cathy, Cheryl, Karen, and Vicky came back. The happy feelings came back. He remembered the day the girls dressed him up as a girl and made him 'one of the girls'.

For just a few minutes, he could forget all the pain of being a boy and hating it. He his mind went to the days he was a girl and loving it. He thought of the dozens of other things he enjoyed doing with all the girls he knew and liked over the few years of his brief life.

Here was this little oasis in a world of insanity. After about 30 minutes, Rex got back into his pajamas and went to a relaxed peaceful sleep. The first he had in months.

Every few nights, Rex would go back into the bathroom, lock the door, and dress in his mother's clothes. When he did, he would feel a calm, a sense of happiness, even joy.

It felt like it did when he was being hugged by his mom and his dad. He just felt right. He realized he was always a girl inside. Dressing was one of the few ways that he could still experience being a girl.

COOKING

One day, Rex's mother was having one of her down days, when she was crying all the time, and had just boiled up some macaroni—for the third time that week.

Rex whined. "Macaroni again? We had that last night!"

"Fine, make your own dinner" Lois and ran into her bedroom crying.

Rex had read a few books on cooking and had watched his mom cook. He would even help. He found some hot dogs in the refrigerator, got a pan, and filled it with hot water. When the water boiled, he put in 4 hot dogs in and waited 5 minutes for them to cook.

He got out some buns and used a pair of tongs to fish out the hot dogs before dumping the boiling water into the sink. Since mom had been crying, Rex gave two of the hot dogs to his mom and ate one himself. He brought the cooked hot dogs.

"Here mommy, these are for you. I put ketchup on them and everything!"

Lois cried even more.

Rex asked, "Did I do something bad?".

She fought back the tears. "I'm crying because I'm so proud of you! I'm going to teach you how to cook!".

Rex smiled big and nodded. "That would be wonderful!"

Over the next few months, Rex and his mother did a lot of cooking. He learned to make spaghetti, chili, hamburgers, hot dogs, and helped mom make stew and pot roast. He also learned to bake cookies and muffins.

Rex also helped Lois sort the laundry. He folded the clothes when they were dry. Sometimes, his mom would even let him vacuum. When he was sick with Asthma, she taught him to knit and to sew by hand. Rex even repaired one of his favorite stuffed animals, performing "surgery" with a needle and thread. Rex even made some doll clothes for his sister's baby doll.

GRANDMA'S CELLAR

That summer, Rex was spending the week with his grandparents. It had been a quiet afternoon, and Rex went into their bedroom. Rex had become quite adept at sneaking into his mother's drawers and making sure that no one knew he had done it. It was almost like being an undercover spy like James Bond or the Man from Uncle, or Mission Impossible.

Rex investigated his grandmother's bottom drawer and found a full figure corset, complete with white lacing and a satin panel in front. Rex had seen them in the sears catalog and wondered if it would make him feel more like a girl. He liked how it felt, but it was too big. He tried to put it back exactly as he had found it.

The next day, Rex went back into his grandmother's room and opened the bottom drawer. He just felt the satin on the front panel and prayed to God, "Make me a pretty girl".

He hadn't heard his grandmother come in. She had suspected that Rex was getting into her dresser, but couldn't imagine why.

The prayer of a little boy had told her everything. She had taken care of Rex many times since he was a baby. When she gave him a bath, she saw the bruises. She had taught Sunday School and watched Rex play with the other girls. He seemed to enjoy playing with his cousins Beth, Carol, Laurie, and Linda. When he played with Steve or Rick, he ended up getting hurt, or locked into a closet, and often ended up crying so badly he got asthma. Now it all made sense.

She bent down to Rex and laughed. "You don't want to play with those ugly old lady clothes."

She smiled a bigger smile than usual. "Come with me, I've got a something I want to show you!"

She held Rex's hand and walked him down to the cellar. It was down the back porch and down the stairs. There were jars of canned fruit in one room, but then she used a hidden key to open another door and there were a bunch of clothes. As Rex looked closer, he realized that these were beautiful dresses.

Grandma was almost wistful. "These are the dresses your mom and your aunts wore to weddings, proms, dances, and special church events. If you like, you can play down here as much as you want, and no one will bother you. It will be our little secret, OK? We don't want to upset Grandpa!"

Then she pulled down another hidden key from inside. "When you play in here, lock yourself in so no one disturbs you."

Rex couldn't believe his ears. He gave his grandma an enormous hug.

"Thank you, grandma, I love you SO MUCH!"

He cried, but they were tears of joy. For the first time in his life, someone knew he was a girl, and loved him anyway.

Rex spent most of his free time down in the cellar, trying on various dresses. He even took off his boy clothes so he could feel the taffeta, chiffon, and other pretty fabrics. It was like Rex had found heaven.

Lois had been struggling with her pregnancy and taking care of the kids, so Rex was spending a lot of time with his grandparents, especially when the cousins came to visit.

One week, his cousin Beth came to visit. Rex was down in the cellar trying on a dress when Beth came in and saw him.

She giggled. "You look really pretty. If you had longer hair, you would be a pretty girl."

The rest of the afternoon, they tried on the various dresses. Beth told him about different colors and fabrics, and they giggled and laughed together.

When his cousin Linda came, she also found Rex in the cellar. She also thought Rex was pretty. They played in the cellar together for the entire week. Linda also let Rex play with her Barbie dolls.

One day, Linda brought down her brother, Mark. Mark also wanted to try on the clothes. They were all giggling together, and Mark gave Rex a big hug and a kiss on the cheek.

The cousins would go down to the cellar on rainy days. They would get dressed and have tea parties. Sometimes, they would sing Sunday school songs. They would giggle and laugh together.

Some of the other cousins weren't so nice. They went up to a cabin and the of his cousins, Steve, Rick, and David, locked Rex and Mark into a cellar so they could play with Beth. Scared, Rex and Mark cuddled with each other. By the time Aunt Liz found them, both were in tears and couldn't stop sobbing.

Rex learned Rick had a cruel streak. He seemed to enjoy making Rex suffer in strange and unusual ways. Rick was smart and sneaky, too. He would lock Rex into the garage, a closet, or tie him up and blindfold him. Rick seemed to take pleasure in not the physical pain, but watching others suffer emotional pain. He would say terrible things that he was going to do. To watch the panic on their faces. Rex was a favorite target.

Rex tried to avoid being alone with Rick. He also kept an extra skeleton key hidden in the cellar, where Rick would sometimes lock up Rex for hours. Little did Rick know, Rex was only pretending to be terrified at being locked up in that cellar. It meant that he would be undisturbed for 3-4 hours, because Rick would try to dissuade anyone from going down there, sometimes by threatening to lock them up.

Linda was excited to tell Rex a secret. "When cousin David was here, we played dress up too. He even wanted to wear panties. He was so cute! He wanted to be a girl too!"

Everybody knew they had to keep the secret. Grandpa wasn't to even know the dresses existed, because he would burn the prom dresses if he knew what they were. Grandpa thought dancing was a sin and had taken a strap to the girls for trying to go to a dance.

In fact, when Lois, the youngest, went to her prom, they had to sneak her out. She had to go to Uncle Alec's, change there, and change back into her nightie so she could look like she had been sleeping. She even had to climb a ladder to get back into her room.

SECOND GRADE

The summer went by quickly. Lois took him to beginner swimming lessons. After having a major episode of runny nose, his instructor told him he had to wear nose plugs in the pool.

Rex had learned breath control, front float, and back float, as well as kicking and basic, simple strokes.

His parents got him a bigger bicycle. They rode with him on the riding trail along cherry creek for a couple miles. Then they saw a dead rattlesnake shot with a gun. Tom told Rex he couldn't ride his bike on the trail alone.

In August, Lois measured Rex for his school clothes. She measured his waist, butt, chest, arms, and inseams. Both Lois and Tom had grown up during the depression. Tom had not received an expected promotion at work. As a result, funds were tight.

"Lois, order Rex's clothes a couple of sizes larger than his current sizes. Hopefully, he won't outgrow them before the end of the school year."

Lois ordered the clothes from the Sears Roebucks catalog over the phone.

When the clothes arrived, they looked ridiculous. Lois had to roll up the cuffs on his pants by over four inches. Rex needed a belt because his pants fell off without one. His shirt tails were so long that his shirt almost looked like a dress. The sleeves on the flannel shirts had to be rolled up several inches as well.

His winter coat went to half-way down his calf. It should have come to his thighs, but looked more like an old man's overcoat. Even his sweaters had to be rolled up.

Rex didn't like the clothes. Not because they looked ridiculous, which they did, but because they were boys' clothes. They were uncomfortable! The pants scratched, and the shirts itched.

Rex wouldn't have to ride the bus this year. He would walk to a local school less than a mile away. He hoped that Vicky and Karen would walk to school with him.

The first day of school started horribly. It was a warm day. Not a great day to be wearing oversized blue jeans, a flannel shirt, and tie-up oxford shoes. Rex got to school early, but everybody had to wait outside until the first bell rang.

The 6th graders who worked as crossing guards impressed Rex. They had orange belts around their waist and over their shoulder. They helped the kids cross the street in safety.

When the first bell rang, everybody had to go to their assigned rooms. Rex was disappointed to find that his friend from church went elsewhere.

As they walked into the room, the kids found tent cards with their names on them taped to each desk. The names were in alphabetical order. Rex was in the third seat on the left side of the room. Each desk had a surface that lifted to put books, supplies, and papers inside.

"Good morning class! My name is Mrs. Kerr. I'm going to be your second-grade teacher. I know many of you went to a different school last year. This is a new school, so we will do everything together. I will take you to lunch, to recess, and to gym class. I also will walk you to the bathrooms. Another teacher will teach music while I teach her class math. Are there questions?"

The class was silent.

"Let's see what you did this summer. How many of you read books during the summer?"

Most of the kids raised their hands.

"How many of you read over 5 books?"

Fewer kids raised their hands.

"How many of you read over 10 books?"

Only five girls and two boys raised their hands, including Rex.

"How many of you read over 20 books?"

Only two girls and Rex had their hands up.

Mrs. Kerr pointed to the first girl. "What is your name and how many books did you read?"

"My name is Missy and I read 25 books!"

The teacher pointed to the second girl. "Who are you and how many did you read?"

"My name is Cristy and I read 27 books!"

Mrs. Kerr pointed to Rex. "Well, young man, how many did you read?"

"My name is Rex and I read 43 books!"

Mrs. Kerr stared, stunned. "Where did you get all these books?"

"My dad took me to the library. Every week, I could check out six books. After reading them all, I would get six new books. I did that every week all summer long."

The teacher did the math. "Wait, you read six books a week all summer? That's over 60 books!"

"Well, several of the books were non-fiction books I liked, so I read them again."

Mrs. Kerr had read Rex's file. She had been told that even though Rex was intelligent, he seemed to act dumb. Now she realized Rex was going to be bored to tears in second grade.

"OK class, I want each of you to write a story telling me what you did this summer. Include anything you did on vacation and any hobbies or things you like doing. I'll give you 40 minutes to write your story."

She handed out ruled paper on which the kids would write their stories.

Ten minutes later, Rex raised his hand.

"Yes, Rex? Are you done?"

"No. I was wondering if I could have another piece of paper?"

Ten minutes later, Rex filled the second sheet, and he was requesting another.

"I'll give you three more sheets. That should last you."

By the end of the assignment, Rex had filled all 5 sheets of paper on both sides. His penmanship was bad, but the story was readable.

"OK class, hand your stories forward."

There was a ruffling of papers as they passed them forward.

"Now class, I will take you to use the bathrooms. You will have ten minutes. You need to do your business, wash your hands and leave. We will wait in the hall then walk back to class together."

When Rex entered the bathroom, he was a bit surprised. On the right side of the room was a long tank about 16 feet long. On the left side, there were only four stalls and none of them had doors. In the center was a long semicircular sink with four soap dispensers.

Rex went to the far end of the long trench. The other boys peed into it. Rex tried to fumble with the zipper on his oversized pants, then had to move the long shirttails of the flannel shirt out of the way. He tried to reach through the fly of his oversized jockey shorts.

Jimmy shouted out. "Whatsa matter SISSY! Can't you find it! Even if you did, it's too short to get through all those layers."

Rex was getting frustrated. "It won't pop out. I'm afraid I'll pee all over my clothes!"

The other boys started laughing.

"Finally!" Rex sighed as he directed the flow into the trench.

Just then, Scotty bumped into him.

Rex said, "You made me pee on my clothes!"

Rex went to the sink. The errant stream had already wet his hands. He pushed the foot control and tried to catch a small stream from a few of the flows that were working. Then he pushed the soap dispenser.

"What is this stuff? It feels like SAND!"

"Jimmy laughed. Well SISSY, that's Borax-o. It's soap that will remove even the worst kind of dirt. It even cleans off engine grease!"

Rex tried to wash off his hands, but his hands still felt gritty and dirty even after then he rinsed them off.

Rex was the last one out of the bathroom and lined up with the rest of his class. As they walked back, another class was walking toward the bathrooms.

This was because the peak period of the baby boom was all in elementary school. They built the school for 400 students, but there were 600 students in the school. Rex's year was one of the largest grades.

Mrs. Kerr then led the class into the Gymnasium. This was an enormous room, just large enough for a basketball court. The kids were told to sit in the same order as they did in class.

"I'm Mrs. Gifford. I'll be your gym teacher this year. Depending on the weather, you will either play outside or you will play inside doing exercises. When we play outside, the boys will play kickball or softball in the field or soccer in Garland Park. We require you to stay with your class and I will decide who will go where."

"Girls will either play on the blacktop or the playground, and will have their choice of hopscotch, four-square, tether-ball, swings, rings, or bars."

The President's Council on Physical Fitness funded the gym program. Its primary goal was to prepare boys to where they would be ready for military service within six weeks of being drafted.

"Today, I will give the boys a soccer ball. You will go play on the soccer field. You can play until I blow my whistle or until the bell rings, whichever comes first. How many boys know how to play soccer?"

Five of the boys raised their hands.

"Good. You will teach the rest of the boys how to play. There are nets for goals in the field. Girls, you will follow me out to the blacktop. I can teach you any games you don't already know how to play."

When they got to the field, 2 of the boys, Jimmy and Scotty, were captains and picked members of their teams. Each took turns. Rex was the last person not yet picked.

Jimmy growled, "Fine! We'll take the SISSY, but you have to give us 5 points!"

Scotty laughed. "Done! I would have given you 7!"

In less that 10 minutes, one boy from his own team had tripped Rex. 14 out of 16 boys started kicking him.

Jimmy cheered. "We each have to kick him 5 times!"

The year was off to a rocky start.

Meanwhile, while her class was at Gym, Mrs. Kerr was curious about the boy who read so many books and had written so many pages. She rifled through the stack of papers. She found the first page with Rex's name on it. Then she noticed someone had shuffled the other pages into the papers for that row. Rex had written his first name on the top of each page.

The penmanship appalled her. Rex was left-handed. The penciled writing on the left side of the page smeared toward the left. Some letters were backward, but it wasn't always consistent. Others looked like attempts at cursive. The sentence structure was typical of a second grader. Short sentences of a few words each.

What surprised her, though, was the vocabulary of the writing. Rex was WRITING words that were far above the reading capabilities of most third graders. There were even scientific terms and cooking terms that were unusual for any elementary school student.

In the writing, Rex understood elementary mathematics. He had done addition and had even done some simple multiplication. When Mrs. Kerr questioned his reading, he admitted she was right about the 60 books, but explained he had read a few more than once and therefore couldn't be double-counted.

Jean Kerr realized it would only be a matter of time before class would bore Rex.

When Mrs. Kerr came to lead her class back to her room, she noticed Rex was limping. He was holding his sides and was holding his shirt closed. Since she had walked them to the gym, she could see that someone had attacked Rex. As they walked back, she heard some boys taunting him. She turned back, held her finger to her lips and hushed the class. "We don't talk when we are walking down the halls."

They had math next. Each student had a book of math drills. They had to copy the math problems to a lined sheet of paper and then write the answers to each.

Mrs. Kerr noticed Rex wasn't writing at all. It was like he couldn't even lift his arms. He was wincing in pain. For about 15 minutes, he just stopped writing and looked out the window. It was like he was a thousand miles away, or at least in the mountains he could see from the window.

After math, Mrs. Kerr led her class to the lunchroom. Many kids brought their own lunch. Others purchased their lunches from the lunch line. They paid 25 cents for a plate comprising a protein, a bread, a vegetable, and a starch, all ladled up from vats of food. It wasn't fancy, but it was nutritious and warm.

When Rex left the line to sit down, the boys refused to let him sit with them, and the girls refused to let him sit with them. He found a spot at the end of his class's assigned table, sitting alone.

Rex ate his meal as quickly as he could, then took his tray and dishes to the window where they would got washed. He was the first to be done with lunch. He was then told to go out to the blacktop.

When he got to the blacktop, Mrs. Gifford recognized Rex from his long, thin body and oversized clothes, but even more so from his limp. It wasn't just his leg that was hurting. He struggled with each step and his pain included his legs, his thighs, his flanks, and his back.

Rex, why don't you play four-square with the girls. They will teach you how.

It took a few turns for Rex to understand how to play the game. Once he understood the game, he did his best to play nice. Some other boys joined the game, and they played to win. They hit Rex with the ball.

Rex just sat inside a windowsill and watched others play. He saw girls playing jump rope with a single rope, but he was still in too much pain to jump.

All Rex wanted to do was get back to class.

Eventually, the bell rang. Rex got into the hallway and lined up behind Mrs. Kerr. She led them back to class.

The next class was music. The Music teacher came into the room as Mrs. Kerr left.

"Hi Class, I'm Mrs. Nordstrom. I'll be your music teacher. I will teach you to sing. We'll start out with some simple songs.

She led them through the songs, teaching them by rote. Rex recognized them as songs he had sung in church. Several times, he kept singing when the class had stopped. This let to giggles throughout the class.

"That's very good Rex. It seems you know this song, but could you wait until I teach it to the rest of the class?"

This led to even more giggles and a threat from the boy sitting behind and to the left.

When music class was over, Mrs. Kerr came back and the next section was on history. There was a book that had very simplified stories of historical figures. As soon as the lesson started, Rex read the entire chapter while the teacher read to the class at a slower pace.

Rex started getting bored and was staring out the window.

Mrs. Kerr hoped to get him back to taking part in the class.

"Rex, who was the first President of the United States?"

Rex didn't even bother to take his eyes off the mountains.

"George Washington."

The lesson continued until Mrs. Kerr told the class to line up for recess.

She led them out to a small playground. There were swings, an arch with horizontal rungs, rings, and a small slide.

The teacher taught them to play "Red Rover" and the entire class played. It was a good way for the class to learn on each other's names.

CAUGHT IN THE ACT

One day, after a terrible day at school, Rex had gone into the bathroom and locked himself in so he could get dressed up. He had put on everything he could, including his mom's girdle, slip, and dress. It was way too big on Rex's little body, but it gave Rex a few moments of peace.

He fell to his knees and prayed as hard as he could. "Please god, make me a girl", he did this over and over, and lost track of time.

He heard a knock on the door and his mother called out, "Rex, what are you doing in there? Are you OK?".

Rex called back, "I'm sitting on the potty!"

He tried to get out of the clothes, but his mother heard the commotion and thought maybe Rex was doing something bad, like playing with matches or something.

Lois got a hanger from the closet, and in just a few seconds, opened the door. Rex couldn't reach for the zipper. He couldn't get out of the dress.

Lois was in shock. She just stood there and stared, her mouth wide open, and her eyes wide.

Rex thought of Cathy's mother and how she freaked out. He began crying, sobbing, out of control.

His mom would throw him out!

Or hate him.

She could call him evil.

Or worse.

Maybe she wouldn't love him anymore!

Lois took Rex into her bedroom and held him close as he cried himself out. Rex sobbed "please don't hate me!".

Lois held him even closer and kissed the top of his head.

"Don't be silly, you are my child and I love you."

Rex cuddled in closer and hugged Lois. He stopped sobbing, wondering what would happen next.

Lois looked at Rex. He had tried to wear everything she had worn to church that morning, and he was trying to dress the way he saw her dress.

Lois had heard the stories of Christine Jorgensen. Was Rex like her?

She held Rex tighter. "Why don't you tell me why you are wearing all of my clothes?".

Rex whimpered. "I like the way they feel, and I enjoy being pretty, like the girls at school and at church."

Lois tried to encourage him. "Yes, they feel nice, don't they? Do you like looking like a girl?"

Rex almost broke down again. "I want to be a girl so bad, mom. I hate being a boy! I hate playing with the boys! I wish I could play with the girls like I used to. Can't I just grow my hair out and be like the rest of the girls? Please mom! If I am forced to keep being a boy, I think I'll die!".

Lois thought back. She realized it was true. Rex was a girl inside. He loved playing with girls. Rex even played like a girl. He even enjoyed doing girl stuff and "woman's work", like helping with the cooking and the cleaning and the laundry.

She held him and tried to calm him. "I'll tell you what. Tomorrow we'll go shopping and maybe get you some tights and a skirt, so you can at least be a girl at home. Would that be nice?".

Rex looked into his mother's eyes. He couldn't believe what he was hearing. "Really, mom? I would like that so much. Even just a few girl clothes would be so nice! I just wish I could play with the girls, too."

Tom came in and just stopped in his tracks. He had been watching a television show and came in when it was over because he had heard the crying. Tom looked at Rex, in his wife's clothes, and just had a blank stare on his face. He was in shock.

Lois turned to Tom. "Tomorrow I'm going to take Rex shopping for some girl clothes."

Tom just nodded. "Keep it under ten bucks."

That night, Tom and Lois sat on the bed and had a serious talk. Tom had seen how distraught Rex was. He had given Rex enough baths to know about the bruises he got at school. He also knew that Rex was more than a little feminine and liked to play with girls.

His concern surprised Lois. "I was much like Rex when I grew up, weak, sick, and feminine. I'm worried that giving him girls' clothes might create false hope. It might make the bullying even worse."

Lois chuckled. "Funny, isn't it? You grew up all feminine and had a bunch of girl buddies. I was the tomboy who beat polio so I could play baseball and ride bicycles with the boys. My uncle Lloyd was feminine too."

Lois changed tracks. "I promised him a shopping trip. I'll just tell him we have a small budget. When I see my therapist on Tuesday, I'll talk to him about this. Let's see what options might be available."

The next day, Lois took Rex to Sears and took him to look at underwear and Rex saw a pair of blue tights that were shiny. Rex looked at pretty acetate panties.

Lois said, "I'll get you a pair of cotton ones. This package has pink, blue to match your tights, and white. Tell you what, instead of spending what's left on a skirt, we can make one at home."

Lois also picked out a scoop-neck blouse that matched the tights.

When they got home, Lois said, "We'll make a wrap skirt so you can wear it and fold it up."

Lois grabbed two yards of red fabric she had been saving for a dress. She put it together with the seams at the tie. Then she had Rex do the hem by hand.

"That way you can make it shorter or longer."

When Tom came home, Rex couldn't wait to show his daddy his new outfit.

Tom smiled. "Wow, you look pretty, but let me show you something."

Tom untied the skirt and tied it around Rex's shoulders. "If anyone makes fun of you, you can turn it into a cape and be a hero like Superman."

Tom deflated Rex, "Don't you want me to be a pretty girl?".

Tom sighed, "I just don't want you getting hurt anymore."

Tom teared up. He walked to the bedroom and cried.

CONVERSION THERAPY

The next day, Lois went to talk to her psychologist.

"My son, Rex, wants to be a girl. I think he might be like Christine Jorgensen. How can we help him?".

The doctor's mouth just dropped. He shook his head. "This is terrible, Lois. Christine Jorgensen had to go to Denmark to get her treatments and surgery. Here in the United States, it's illegal for a doctor to perform that kind of surgery. He can't even give a boy female hormones."

Lois gasped, almost in panic. "Is there anything we can do to help him or her? She's suffering in school."

The doctor hoped to calm Lois.

"Yes, we call this Gender Identity Disorder. It's a psychosis, like schizophrenia. In the 1950s, Dr Robert Galbraith Heath suggested one treatment for such disorders. It comprises a daily program of electroshock therapy, aversion therapy including electrocution of the genitalia while watching stimulation to be avoided, and sleep deprivation—for about 3 months."

Lois' eyes filled with hatred and horror.

"I've BEEN through daily electroshock therapy! Just like you just described. Do you know how HORRIBLE that is?"

Her voice went cold, menacing.

"Minutes of agony as every muscle in your body cramps and convulses all at once. You pass out from the pain. Then you wake up with feelings of terror and fear. You're unable to remember where you are, why you are there. You're unable to stand, unable to eat. Then you feel horrible for hours."

Her voice calmed. "When it happens day after day, it destroys your mind. I've lost three years of my son's life. I can't remember anything that happened since I got pregnant until Rex was two years old."

She looked straight into the doctor's eyes.

"Do you think for one minute that I would let anyone do that to my little boy?!!"

The doctor held his hand up. "Let's hope that won't be necessary. What you should know is that in severe cases of Gender Identity Psychosis, this delusion of being the wrong gender becomes so intense that the subject may resort to extreme measures, getting castrated, or even committing suicide. They reach the point where they literally cannot live with the reality of spending the rest of their life in their male body."

"Freud explained a girl who wanted to be a boy as having 'penis envy', but the psychiatric community figures that no man in his right mind would want to give up the privileges of being a man, therefore it must be a psychosis."

The doctor laughed at his own joke, but Lois wasn't laughing.

Lois stared in horror. Would Rex end up locked up in a padded cell, unable to function in society? "What happens if the other treatments don't work?" She dreaded the answer.

The doctor leaned forward and spoke. "Lois, if your son is severe as he sounds, and the other treatments don't work, there is a very good chance they would have to perform a lobotomy. It would not turn him into a complete zombie, but it would wipe most of what makes him your son. He might not even remember who you are."

The doctor rushed to continue. "It could be much worse. Many lose all hope of being OK in their own bodies. They see reincarnation as their only option. For many, they decide it is better to eliminate this body and move on to the next. To the rest of the friends and family, it looks like suicide or an accidental death."

The odds are that if you don't get him the treatments, your son will be dead before he is 20. Your best hope is to get him to accept his body and at least attempt to masquerade as a boy as best as he can.

The next day, Rex went to Barry's house and showed off his new skirt and tights. Barry made fun of Rex and so Rex pulled off the skirt and wore it like a cape. Rex realized he couldn't trust even his best friends. He could trust nobody.

Rex wore the tights under his pants for six weeks, running them to where he couldn't even find the legs.

"Mom! Can I get another pair of tights? The ones you bought me have fallen apart. Can I get some new ones?"

"Your father doesn't want you spending any more money on clothes you can't wear." She couldn't bear to tell Rex that he could never be a girl.

EVASION

Second Grade was worse than ever. Rex had to walk to school. He could walk to the major streets, but when he did, the boys would chase him and hit him with sticks and rocks. The other route was through a vacant lot where there were rattlesnakes. Rattlesnakes were the safer route.

When school let out, Rex was walking down the street. He had just crossed Holly and was about to cross Cherry Creek.

"Hey SISSY! You left too soon! A bunch of us BOYS wanted to be here when you walked home!"

"Yeah! We wanted you to meet the CLUB!"

"Well, we wanted you to meet the CLUBS! Get him!"

Rex tried to run, but he couldn't run fast enough. They were off school grounds. Mrs. Gifford couldn't blow her whistle. Mrs. Kerr couldn't call the class in. They could take as long as they wanted.

"Hey SISSY! Don't you like us?" WHAM! The club landed behind his right knee. Then another hit his back.

"Oh SISSY! You're a bombing nation, we should kill you right now!"

"Nobody can save you now, SISSY! We can hit you for as long as we want."

Just then, a man stopped his car in the middle of the street.

"Hey! What are you boys doing! Leave her alone!"

The boys stopped. "We can get you any time we want SISSY!"

For weeks, Rex couldn't sleep. He couldn't fall asleep at night. When he fell asleep, he had horrible nightmares about his beatings. Often, he would be awake until 2AM and be up at 6AM to watch the sunrise.

About the only time he got a good night's sleep was when he got dressed up, but even that didn't always work.

Rex figured out that if he didn't do his written work during class, the teacher would make him stay and do it after school.

"What I hate most about math is that I have to copy the numbers and problems from the book onto the paper before I can write the answers. I could write the answers in the book in about 5 minutes."

Mrs. Kerr could see Rex racked with pain when he came back from gym. Some days, he couldn't even lift his arms to the desk. Staring out the window seemed to be his only relief from the pain.

"I know it's frustrating for you, Rex. Unfortunately, you must copy the problems just like all the other students. The school board won't pay for math books for students every year. You can do it after class, but you have to do it."

"It's OK Mrs. Kerr! This way, I don't have to run away from the boys who beat me up on the way home. If I take long enough, they will be in their houses eating!"

"So THAT'S why you listen to the lectures for both sides of the class, and then wait until after school to finish your written work. And I thought you might be dumb."

"I like it here at night. The only nasty part is listening to that magic marker! The squeaking is almost like fingernails on a chalkboard. At least I'm not getting hit."

"I'm just curious Rex, what books are you reading these days?"

"Here's one I'm reading now!"

Rex pulled out a book he had picked at the library.

"Let me see. That's a big book! There are some hard words in there? Can you read all of them?"

"Oh yes! Those words are easy. I like to read about dinosaurs, reptiles, electricity, electronics, and mechanics."

"How do you find children's books about electronics and mechanics?"

"Oh! I got bored with the children's section. Now I get most of my books from the Young Adult section of the library. Sometimes dad takes me to University Hills, other times we go to Cherry Creek."

"I'll tell you what, Rex. I want you to right me a one page book report on each book you read. It can be longer, but I want to discuss the book with you at night. Would you like that?"

"Well. I guess that would be OK. But do I have to use that kiddie paper? Can I use a full size tablet? Do I have to limit it to one page?"

"Fine! You can use a wide-ruled tablet and use as many pages as you like. Do your writing at home, but you can bring it to class and we can discuss it at night!"

"That sounds like fun!"

Mrs. Kerr would read the reports and talk about the books Rex was reading. Rex understood the books. He could also make logical conclusions.

PARENT TEACHER CONFERENCE

Jean Kerr called a parent/teacher conference with both of Rex's parents. She wanted to know what they knew and see if they could help their son.

"Thank you both for coming. I wanted to talk to you about several issues to make sure we are on the same page."

"Which issues are those?"

"First. Rex is very intelligent. He's told me you have been taking him to the library. He's been reading a lot of books. Do you have a list of the books he's read?"

Tom spoke, "Oh yes! I list all the book titles when we come home. If he loses one, it's easier to find it when you know what you're looking for. Lois checks off the ones that he has read. He has to read them before we will take him back to the library."

"These are young adult books?"

"Yeah, I know, he should read children's books, but he doesn't like fiction books much, and there aren't many non-fiction books in the children's section."

"No, that's fine! If he can read at Young Adult level, that's a remarkable accomplishment. Do you help him read the books?"

"Lois helps him with some of the hard words if they are new. He's pretty good at sounding them out."

"I think we bore Rex with class. He very often just looks out the window. Sometimes I'll ask him questions to get his attention. He'll answer the questions correctly without ever taking his eyes off the window."

"He's probably looking at the mountains. He was the same with television. He'd watch the news with Tom for an hour. He looked like he was just staring into space. Then he would ask questions about the stories."

"Wait! He watches the news with you? And you talk about it afterword?"

"He loves Walter Cronkite. I think he reminds Rex of his grandfather."

"Moving on. I think Rex is struggling with writing. He writes left-handed. Is he always left-handed?"

"Well, he eats, writes, colors, knits, crochets, and sews left-handed. He hammers nails right-handed."

"I'm amazed! Rex can all those things? I assume you taught him? Lois. How did you teach him?"

"I'm right-handed, so I sat across from him and had him do what he saw. He would simply mirror whatever I was doing. He would pick it up in a matter of minutes. He gets lots of practice in the hospital."

"That's the next item. After gym, lunch, and recess, he seems to be in a lot of pain. Do you have any idea why?"

"Those are his least favorite subjects. He often comes home crying. He's been better since he started staying after school."

Tom said, "I help him with his bath. I wash his back. It's hard as a father to see my son's body covered with bruises. Often, he has bruises from his ankles to his wrists."

Lois nodded. "He wakes up screaming almost every night. Sometimes I'm reading or knitting, and I'll hear him screaming in terror. He's afraid to go to sleep. He'll often be up well past midnight."

"Yes, and he is often wide awake before I even get out of bed to go to work. I've gone to the bathroom only to see him staring out the window, waiting for the sunrise I guess."

"He says that the boys kick him when he goes out to play soccer. Rex has to play with them, even though he is the last one picked. Each time they play, one of his own teammates will trip him."

Tom mused. "I can't imagine what it must be like. He knows he has to go to school, and he knows he will get kicked and punched at least twice before he gets home."

"Rex says both teams like to play Kick the Sissy!"

Mrs. Kerr understood. "That explains why he has been late getting back to class. Sometime Rex will be in so much pain that he can't move. He just must have just laid there and cried after the bell rang. He can barely lift his arms."

Lois wiped her eyes. "In the hospital, he learned to stare at a specific point while they gave him IVs. He has learned to use this with some intense physical and emotional pain."

"Several times Mrs. Gifford has come out to the field and helped him to the nurse's office. She's stopped making up lies about how Rex came by so many bruises, and just said 'Again!'. It's happening every day."

Lois blotted her eyes. "By the time he gets to the Nurse's Office, he is already wheezing. I've already had to take him to the hospital three times last year and twice this year. He's already got VIP status. The first time he went in last year, the doctor almost called the police."

"Even this year, he had to explain to the doctors that we weren't hurting him. He said that ALL the boys had hurt him. He even listed their names, but begged the doctor not to tell anyone, because they would hurt him worse."

Over the next 6 years, Rex would be hospitalized 60 more times.

EMERGENCY ROOMS

Lois got another call from the school nurse. Rex was crying and was having an asthma attack.

"Mrs. Gifford had to carry him in. He couldn't move, and his asthma was terrible. He's wheezing."

Rex was in terrible shape when Lois arrived. His fingernails were turning blue. His lips were turning white. He couldn't talk.

Lois gave him his inhaler. "We'll be at the hospital in about 20 minutes. Just keep breathing!" It was such a struggle. Rex wanted to just fall asleep and stop trying. It hurt so much to breathe, and he knew what was coming. Still, he passed out for the last 10 minutes of the trip.

When they got to the hospital, a nurse pulled Rex out of the car. She laid him on a gurney and shook him awake.

"Hey kiddo, welcome back! You've been away for almost four weeks! Now, what do you need?"

Rex came to just enough to gasp out "10 CC's Eppy, IV, and O2".

The doctor met Rex just as he was being wheeled into the exam room. This was a new resident. He had heard the nurse take Rex's order and said, "Make it 25 CC's Epinephrine".

The doctor pulled back in horror as he raised Rex's shirt. The bruises were getting colorful. It looked like a herd of buffalo or something had trampled Rex. He winced as he pressed the stethoscope to Rex's chest, but Rex didn't even flinch.

"Did your PARENTS do that!?"

Rex smiled and said, "No! They would never hurt me! The boys at school did that."

The doctor couldn't believe his eyes. "How many boys were there?" He couldn't believe that second-grade boys could do that much damage.

Rex choked as he coughed, and then gasped. "About 12 today. Some boys were sick!" He then rattled off a list of names.

The nurse came in with the needle. The doctor nodded, showing to give the shot. Rex was used to this by now. He could relax as the nurse emptied the needle into his arm. It was afterward that he felt the burn and the pain.

Rex went into convulsions, and gagging. He vomited into the little tray they held for him, and he irked out "Too much epinephrine!".

The nurse almost barked at the doctor.

"How much did you give him!".

The doctor told her the dose and her eyes almost popped out.

"Didn't he tell you how much he could take? You're lucky you didn't kill him. He's allergic to it, because he's had it so often, he can't take over 5 millilitres."

The doctor said, "He asked for 10, but I thought he needed more!"

He must be severe if he asked for that much.

Rex sat and convulsed. The nurse brought a warm blanket. Rex couldn't even talk. He kept vomiting until there was nothing left. He kept heaving like there was more to come. Finally, he just fell back onto the bed.

The nurse then told the doctor, "Listen to his heart!".

The doctor could hear the beat racing, but instead of the expected "Thump, Thump, Thump" he heard "Thwish, Thwish, Thwish".

He noted to the nurse, "He has a heart murmur!"

The nurse shook her head. "No, he doesn't! That's the Eppy. Did you check his chart?".

With that, she dropped a folder of papers at least 2 inches thick on the table. The first page of the chart read:

INSTRUCTIONS FROM FAMILY DOCTOR

IF REX IS CONCIOUS, HE WILL TELL YOU
WHAT HE NEEDS.

IF NOT THEN HIS MOTHER WILL KNOW.

IF SHE'S NOT AVAILABLE, THEN CALL ME

BEFORE ADMINISTERING ANY
TREATMENT!

The nurse saw the doctor, humbled and despondent.

"Don't worry doctor, Rex is one of our special patients. Most of us are familiar with the drill. This is your first time. You'll find that he's quite extraordinary."

The strain of the emotional and physical abuse often resulted in asthma attacks so severe that Rex had to be hospitalized. Lois had already called the doctor, and the doctor had already called the hospital. The room was ready when Rex was stable.

Next, the nurse came in to insert the IV needle. The panic on Rex's face was obvious.

Rex was still shaking. "My veins roll out of the way."

The nurse thought she was ready. She made her first attempt. Rex held as still as he could while she tried to catch the illusive vein with the needle. She went through the vein, forming a bruise.

Rex had tears streaming down his cheeks, but he knew that crying, screaming, or squirming would only make it worse. As she made her second and third attempts, he whimpered. He picked a spot on the ceiling and just focused on it as he relaxed. In a matter of seconds, he calmed down. She caught a vein, and it didn't tear. With care, she tried to secure it. She could see the bruises under the paper gown forming on his legs and shins. Rex had already been through enough. It would be a long night, and he knew it.

HOSPITALIZATION

They took Rex up to the room. The staff was setting up an oxygen tent. The tent made of clear plastic. People could see, and they could hear if Rex started choking or anything. There was little Rex could hear besides the mist of the vaporizer.

On the floor, the ward doctor did a quick preliminary exam. He noted the all too familiar cuts and bruises. He noted the wheezing of the asthma. He wondered how Rex could keep coming back to life. This had been his 5th visit since the start of the school year, and it wasn't even Christmas yet.

In the oxygen tent, there could be no television, no radio, no electrical devices of any kind. Nothing that would make sparks.

Because Rex was in a tent breathing Isuprel mist, getting IV Adrenalin or Epinephrine, and other drugs to stimulate his heart and breathing, there was little chance of sleeping for more than brief naps. The highlights were the daily lab work and inhalation therapy with the nebulizer. The drugs often caused nausea, vomiting, convulsions, and sometimes even a heart murmur. Without them, the Asthma would turn into pneumonia, or worse.

There were bruises near vital organs. They would have to keep Rex for at least two weeks to heal damage to his liver, kidneys, spleen, or other vital organs.

Lois put her head through the tent and gave Rex a gentle hug. "I brought your crochet hooks and some yarn. I also brought you 6 books. Tomorrow, I will pick up 6 more. I also brought a new brain teaser."

Rex smiled, still shaking. "I'll need them. It's will be a long night. Can you bring a needlepoint kit? I'll make a sweater vest tonight and read the books. Can you bring some fiction books? Maybe a Nancy Drew mystery?"

Lois laughed. "Wow! Fiction books? Is something wrong?"

Rex smiled. "On long nights like these, I like fiction because it takes much longer to read. It's like I'm in the book, and I enjoy pretending I'm Nancy. I've solved it before she gets trapped or tied up."

Rex knitted until about 5:00 AM and fell asleep. Of course, the nurse woke him up at 6:30 AM to take his vitals.

About 10 AM, the tech came in with an enormous machine on a rolling cart. Rex smiled.

"Hi Amos! Time for the gas mask?"

The tech smiled. He was a sweet man, with ebony skin, a friendly smile, and a way of making Rex feel relaxed. He even made it fun.

Amos laughed, "What are you going to be today, a pilot?"

"Yeah, that way I won't upchuck so quick."

Amos put the facemask over his mouth and nose. Rex started taking deep breaths. He coughed each time he tried to exhale.

Amos just grinned. "That's right. Blow out as much as you can from down here. He pressed on Rex's tiny, flat stomach."

Rex giggled. "Pilot to co-pilot, prepare for take-off!" He blew out as much as he could before filling his lungs again. He'd already learned to breathe from his abdomen and then fill up his chest.

The mist contained concentrated Isuprel. Same as in the oxygen tent all day. With the deep breathing, the concentrated dosage, and the Epinephrine drip, it only took Rex about 15 minutes to upchuck. His stomach was heaving,

Amos held a tray to catch came up. Rex's stomach was empty. There was little there. It sounded like his insides were coming up.

Amos patted his back; "You're doin' great Captain! Ready to go again?"

Rex nodded, put the mask back to his face. He blew out everything he could and took another breath. He hated the vomiting. The yucky tasting mist made it much easier to breathe, and he might even sleep an hour when it wore off. Rex had dry heaves 3 more times before the 30 minutes were over. He might even survive the day.

The process continued for 5 days. They would also throw in some fun surprises like a chest X-ray or two. Sometimes they would suction his nose. It was painful, but made it easier to breathe with his mouth closed. That made it easier to sleep.

They tapered the medicine in the IV drip. Rex could even sleep for two hours, two or three times a day. The nurses could tell that Rex was having some horrible nightmares. Sometimes the nurse would just come in and hold his hand for a few minutes.

On the sixth day, the nurse came in. "Would you like to try some juice?"

Rex was so excited! This meant that he could drink juice and have chicken broth! "Yes, please! May I have some apple juice?"

That day, when Amos came in, Rex pretended he was a "Scuba Diver", putting a tube into his mouth. It held his mouth open, but because he was getting better, and the dose was decreasing, he only had a few short tummy spasms, but the juice stayed down.

Tom brought in books on electricity, radio, and a book about music. Rex read those while he knitted. He'd almost finished his vest. It was white and made of very soft acrylic yarn. There were lots of interesting patterns and designs. Some were accidents, others were just Rex trying to make it prettier.

The seventh day, the doctor came in and pulled up Rex's robe and pressed his belly. By now, Rex's wide hips were protruding. The initial blood tests had shown signs of liver and kidney damage. Now they were returning to normal. They wouldn't have to do surgery.

It took about 2 weeks for the entire process. By then, his lung function was back. The bruising had healed. For a few days, he had a wheelchair. Then a day of monitored walking. They discharged him and sent him home.

Rex had gone to bed that night. The beatings would start all over again tomorrow.

LUNACY

Soon, it got to where each full moon meant either Rex or his mom would be in the hospital. Lois would go to the psychiatric ward for acute depression. Rex would go to Children's hospital to recover from asthma and beatings.

Even as young as four years old, Rex knew when his mother needed to go, often before she did. He would hear her calling for him.

The first time, Rex told Alan's mother, Jan "Mom is calling me, we need to see her".

Jan dismissed him, "Your mom is sleeping in your house, you couldn't possibly hear her."

Rex bolted out the door. "She needs me NOW!".

Jan followed Rex, figuring that once Rex knew his mother was OK, he would let her sleep.

Rex ran up the stairs and saw his mother with both arms bleeding. She had cut her wrists with a broken lightbulb.

She was whispering, "Rex, I can't leave you behind, Rex, Rex, Rex."

Jan walked in and was in shock! She screamed "Lois, what have you done!?!".

Jan told Rex to wait downstairs. She got the bleeding stopped, put a pressure bandage on the gashes, and got her ready to go to the hospital.

About 4 weeks later, Rex again heard his mother calling. This time, there was no argument. When they got to the bedroom, Jan took no chances.

"Rex, you wait here, I'll see if she's OK."

As Jan opened the door, the smell of puke filled the air. She covered the bed with vomited pills!

Rex's mother had tried to overdose on pills and booze. Jan had to take her to the emergency room.

By second grade, one moon, Lois would go, the next moon, Rex would go.

KENNEDY

One day, Rex was having another miserable day at recess. The teacher called the kids in to the classroom.

She was silent.

"Someone shot President Kennedy! Please go straight home and be with your families. You may not have much time left."

Everybody knew Denver was ground zero, surrounded by military bases. If there was to be a nuclear strike, everybody would be dead before their minds could register the bright flash, if they were lucky. They had sent the students home during the Cuban Missile Crisis for the same reason.

By the time Jack Ruby shot Lee Harvey Oswald, Rex was in the hospital again, the asthma so severe that they gave him a room in minutes.

WISHES

For Christmas, Rex asked for some Barbie dolls, so he could play with the other girls. Tom got him an Erector Set, to encourage less girlish pursuits. Rex tried to act grateful. His disappointment was obvious. As was his disappointment in the oversized boy's clothes that would make him look ridiculous until summer.

Rex did like spending time with his dad, and the erector set was fun. There was a motor and some belts and pulleys. They made a windmill together. Tom went off to go grocery shopping and Rex had changed the pulleys so that the windmill was spinning like a fan. Then he put his hand in front of the spinning blades. It surprised Rex when they stopped turning.

When Rex blew out the candles on his birthday cake, he closed his eyes and wished with all his might. "I wish I was a girl!" He blew out the candles. He didn't have to tell anyone his wish. Rex always had the same wish. He wished it a lot.

He'd see the first star of the night and do the little rhyme

Star Light, Star Bright,

First Star I see tonight I wish I may, I wish I might, have the wish I wish tonight. To be a girl, free and light.

Rex also wished for it when he got the wishbone, especially the thanksgiving wish bone from the turkey.

There was a silly song on the radio about a girl in a polka dot bikini. Rex made up his own worlds, but didn't sing it in front of anyone, it went:

I've got an Itsy Bitsy Teeny Weeny

shriveled up and wrinkled peeny

and I wish it would just go away.

That Sunday, Rex went to church with his grandparents. He wore pants and a jacket. Rex behaved well in Sunday school. He helped the teacher tell a bible story. Later, he played with the other girls.

When his grandpa came to pick him up, one parent said, "Rex is such a sweet thing, he'd be such a lovely girl."

As soon as they got home from church, grandpa got out the clippers, pulled off the guard, and shaved every bit of hair off Rex's head. The baby fine hair jammed the clippers and pulled his hair. They cut into his scalp. Rex was screaming and crying. Partly from the pain of the clippers. Much more from the knowledge that he could never grow it long, so he could be pretty. Like the other girls.

It took very little hair for Rex to look like a girl. Even enough to look like a pixie cut, an inch, was enough to cause people to mistake him as a girl, especially in the summer when he wore shorts and colored T-shirts. Every time it happened, he would smile with a deep-down happiness.

The insurance company was getting sick of all these hospitalizations. They insisted he see an allergist. She had been a resident at National Jewish Hospital, working with doctors who were Holocaust survivors. They had assisted Mengele with his tests in Auschwitz. The methods were controversial, but they had made breakthrough discoveries. These doctors held out the hope of a cure or at least a reduction in the number or severity of the asthma attacks.

The allergist decided she needed to run a bunch of scratch tests to find out what Rex was allergic to. She realized he seemed to be allergic to almost everything, in different degrees. The scratch tests weren't that bad. She'd twist a nail setter to make a small round scratch in the skin. Then she'd put a drop of serum in that scratch, one for each allergen. Usually, 10 rows of 10 on the back, then 10 rows of 10 in front.

Suddenly, the Doctor nodded to a nurse. "skin pops".

The nurse needed no further instructions from the doctor as she pulled out a padded board with straps on it. Before Rex realized what was happening, the nurse had strapped down his arm at the wrist, elbow, and shoulder, as the doctor had done the same thing on the other side.

They pulled Rex's arms straight out from his chest, and he couldn't move at all. A few seconds later, they were strapping down his legs and waist. The nurse then held Rex's head so that he couldn't move.

Rex couldn't help but think how pretty she was. She had a white dress that came to about mid-thigh, and hair up in a bun, and lovely eye make-up. Rex looked into her eyes and almost relaxed.

Dr Gamble then turned to Lois.

"You need to stay silent! This will not be pleasant, and he needs to have as few memories of you as possible. I'm going to run some skin-pop tests on the strongest reactions. They feel a bit like bee stings. They can burn for about 30 minutes while we wait for the results to show."

Dr Gamble then injected a bubble of allergen serum just under his skin, like the test for tuberculosis.

Almost immediately, Rex began screaming in pain. "I promise to be good; I'll never get sick again,"

Dr Gamble repeated the process. 2 rows of 9 on each arm, 36 total. Every pop burned like a bee sting, feeling like the skin was on fire. They strapped Rex down for almost an hour to get the final verdict. His skin burning, itching, and causing agonizing pain for the entire time.

That whole week, Rex had nightmares about the pretty nurse and the horrible shots. He woke up screaming. He even dreamed that one of his pretty classmates dressed like the nurse. Other girls were holding him down as she threw darts at him.

The following week, they went through all the scratch tests for about two hours, and the doctor just nodded to the nurse. As soon as Rex saw the arms come out, he fought, knowing what was coming.

They were too fast for him, and soon they strapped him down so he couldn't move. Rex started crying even before the first shot started. There was no way to stop it and no way to escape. By the 12th shot, Rex was screaming in agony, to where he was almost choking.

Lois asked Dr. Gamble, "Is there any way you could give him a sedative or something, so he doesn't have to suffer like this? It just seems so cruel!"

Dr Gamble shook her head. "The doctor who developed brought this technique was a survivor of Mengele's camp. The theory is that if you try to sedate the patient, they will give false negatives. Many begged to be sent to death, but they couldn't quit once they started."

They had to do the skin pops for 5 more weeks, some to confirm discovered results, other times to confirm other allergies. In the middle of the third session, Rex asked the doctor if he could watch her put the needles in so he could hold his arm still.

Rex found it was easier to organize his mind around the pain. It still hurt so badly he wanted to scream. But after watching about 5 of the shots, he had figured out how to focus on holding still for the 5-10 seconds it took to form the bubble. He would then to take several deep breaths before the next shot. The tears would pour out his eyes, but he focused and tried to hold his sound to whimpers and tried to not move his arms at all.

It quite surprised Dr. Gamble at how well Rex had adjusted to the horrible situation. She knew how incredibly painful it was. She knew it had to hurt like torture. Yet Rex had gained control over his emotions and could joke during the scratch tests even though he knew the skin pop tests were coming. He would even smile when the skin pop injections were over. The shots themselves traumatized Rex, but he controlled the trauma.

After each test, however, Rex would have even more nightmares.

After about 10 of these sessions, Dr Gamble suggested no egg yolks for 2 months, and then suggested allergy shots, 4 times a week.

Rex had to go to the doctor's office to get the shots and got three in each arm. He felt like a pincushion and his arms were sore for the next 2 days. Rex had learned to relax his arm enough so that it didn't hurt as bad as it did when he tensed. As an incentive, Rex's parents promised him he could have a pet if he did 3 months' worth of shots.

They got him an iguana, which was a lizard that could grow to up to 6 feet long in a year. The first two iguanas died after only a few weeks. Rex then found out that Iguanas eat crickets and roaches, or maybe a nice juicy grasshopper. Not the lettuce his mom suggested. Rex treated it like a kitty cat. He sang to it, told it stories, and pet its skin. He would even hold the grasshoppers he caught in his hand. That one grew from about 6 inches to over 3 feet long. It died when the heat lamp in its terrarium burned out while the family was visiting his grandparents.

THIRD GRADE

The asthma did not get better, and by third grade, Rex's hospital visits had reached the point where he was going in every 4 weeks for a 2 week stay at the hospital. He was reading at high school level, mostly non-fiction, but math was still a problem. When he was in class, they assigned him a seat next to the window on the "dummy" side of the class. Rex would look up into the mountains and visualize himself among the pine trees, listening to the creek trickling by.

For years, Rex's parents had rented a cabin in the mountains, along with another couple who rented another cabin. Rex's cabin had electricity, but no water. The other cabin had water, but no electricity. At least this way dad got his coffee in the morning, but they still had to heat the cabin with a wood-burning stove. Some of Rex's favorite memories were those of smelling skunk spray. He could smell it from quite a distance away, and when he did, he knew he was in the mountains.

Rex liked to hike in the mountains with another girl. She had lost three of her fingers in a lawn mower accident. She was faster and stronger than Rex, but she loved to show him wonderful sights in the area.

Rex's health would always improve up there, almost from the minute he smelled the skunk. One time, when he was about 4, Rex even tried to catch the bus to the cabin, but the driver didn't know where it was. These were happy memories. And looking at the mountains, he could almost see the pine needles in the trees. He could hear the water running through the creeks.

For Rex, these imaginary visits to the mountains were his way of coping with the acute physical pain of the beatings during gym, lunch, and recess.

The teacher would interrupt these wanderings by asking questions, to which Rex would give an almost trance-like correct answer.

Rex was also staying after school to avoid being bullied by nearly every boy in the school. They filled in the vacant lot, but there were still weeds and snakes. Often, he would sneak through the lots and yards and go out of his way, to avoid the more dangerous gauntlet of the kids on his street.

CUB SCOUTS

"Mommy, I want to join cub scouts! They get to wear uniforms! Since I am older than the rest of them, I'd get to be the first to wear a uniform!"

"Do you know what it's like to be a scout?"

"No, by my friend Anna is already a brownie, and Sarah is a Bluebird. I wish I could be a Bluebird. They have really pretty blue uniforms. Brownie uniforms are just…brown."

"Why don't you got watch TV while your dad and I discuss it."

Rex left the kitchen for the family room.

"Tom, do you really think being a cub scout is a good idea?"

"Well, it's the first time he's actually been excited about anything to do with being a boy. It might be worth a shot."

"I can't help but wonder if this is just a fashion statement. He doesn't have any friends in scouts. We will have to buy the uniform too."

"We should only buy the shirt! I don't want to waste a bunch of money on a full uniform if he's going to drop out in a month."

"Well, at least you can help him earn some merit badges. I assume they aren't too difficult for an 8-year-old."

Rex made it to Bear and earned about a dozen merit badges, including radio, electronics, electricity, photography, crafts, cooking, and several others., but he didn't like the other scouts that much.

SOFTBALL

The last week of school, the scout Den Mother addressed the den.

"There is going to be a softball league and since we only have 10 boys in our den, every boy must play for the season. You'll all get a merit badge for it."

"Even Rex? He's terrible at softball. All he does is stay in the outfield and chase the balls that get past the other fielders. He can't even throw it to the other fielders."

"YES! EVERY boy has to play, and everybody will have to bat, and everybody will have to have to play an actual position."

"Well, we might as well give up every game then."

"Yeah! At school, we usually get 5 or 6 points if we have to take Rex."

At the end of the meeting, the Den Mother pulled Lois aside.

"Is there any chance somebody could work with Rex on his batting skills? He can play outfield, but he needs to at least have a chance of hitting the ball. Maybe his dad could pitch to him?"

Lois laughed loudly at that. "Are you kidding! I'M the tomboy in the family. I'll see if I can teach him to bat."

Lois set up a pole in the yard and tied a ball to it. Rex practiced hitting the ball as it approached him from either side. Soon he could hit it in each direction without it wrapping around the tall pole.

They went to the school playground.

"Since we're just trying to bat, I'm going to stand in front of this backstop and pitch to you. Your dad will catch. I want you to try to hit every ball, no matter where I pitch it. Do you understand?"

"OK mom! I'll try."

He missed the first few pitches, slow and over the plate with no curve. Rex was swinging, but nowhere near the ball.

"I want you to look at the ball and try to see if it's turning toward you or away from you."

Lois tossed the ball several times. Soon Rex was calling each pitch correctly.

"Now I want you to watch the ball the same way, and swing the bat. It may or may not hit the ball. All that matters is that you see the direction and that you swing the bat at the same time."

After about 5 pitches, Rex started hitting every ball that Lois pitched. Even when it came below his knees or above his head, Rex was hitting the ball hard and over his mom's head into the side of the backstop, to his right.

"That's enough for today. You have a game tomorrow. Let's see how it goes."

At the game, Rex was the last boy in the batting order. He played center field, badly. He could stop the ball from rolling past him by throwing his glove at it.

Finally, it was Rex's turn to bat. He hit long high balls, just outside the first base line.

"Wow! Did you see that. Rex just hit the ball 200 feet. If it hadn't been a foul ball, it would have been a home run!"

Rex hit 12 more foul balls. Each over 200 feet. Finally, the pitcher pitched one right at his belly.

"Take your base!"

The next kid hit a line drive right to second base. It was a double play.

By the end of the game, Rex had hit so many foul balls that the kids were calling him "Foul Ball". Each time the pitcher would hit him and they would get him out in a double play.

At his last time at bat, he hit 18 foul balls, then swung and missed. It was the last out of the 9th inning and his team lost.

"We lost, and it's YOUR FAULT SISSY!" Jimmy grabbed a bat and chased Rex.

"Yeah! We would have won if you didn't keep hitting foul balls."

Soon, half the boys on his team were holding bats and chasing Rex. A few times, they swung and missed. By the time the parents, who were watching this, stopped the chase, Tom and Lois were fed up.

"This is what it is to be Scouts? Come on Rex, you don't have to play softball anymore. We're going home."

The Den Mother shouted out. "That's it! You are out of scouts, Rex! You're a little SISSY. Maybe you should join the Bluebirds!"

Rex didn't cry. He didn't even look back.

"Are you upset about leaving scouts?"

"No mom. I'm relieved!"

Scouts opened many interests, including over a dozen hobbies.

FOURTH GRADE

In fourth grade, his teacher was Miss Johnston. On the first day of class, there was a new issue.

"What do you think you are doing, young man!"

She came down on his left hand with a ruler.

"I'm writing. Trying to do your assignment."

She smacked his hand again.

"Why are you using your left hand! Are you evil?"

"No, I'm left-handed."

SMACK!

"You will use your right hand in my class!"

"Yes ma'am, I'll try."

Rex tried to write with his right hand.

SMACK!

"That writing is terrible. Are you still in kindergarten?!"

Rex started to cry. "No ma'am"

Miss Johnston moved on. Picking on other students in the room.

At lunch, Rex had to sit with his class. Despite hostility, he was the least of anyone's concerns.

"Can you believe she HIT us?"

"She's so OLD! She looks like a witch!"

"She just scares me. My hand has bruises!"

"Rex, look at your hands! Both are black-and-blue. Your left hand is bleeding!"

"My mom said that she used to teach at a Catholic parochial school."

"Yeah! My neighbor had her last year. She left the convent to retire. Now she's teaching in a public school."

When Rex got home, he entered quietly. He walked into the family room, but all he could see was the cloud of the smoke.

"Mom? Are you there?"

"Yes Rex, I'm sewing."

He sat down on the couch.

"What happened to your hands? Did the boys beat you?"

"The boys always avoid areas not covered by clothes. My new teacher did this."

"What did she do?"

Rex broke down crying. "She hit me with a ruler! She hit me because I wrote left-handed. I tried to write with my right hand and she hit my hands because my penmanship was so bad. She hit me ten times today! I don't want to go to school anymore!"

"I'll be taking you to school tomorrow. We'll leave early."

When Tom came home, Lois was already in a state.

"Rex's teacher has been hitting his hands with a ruler. His hands were bruised and bleeding! His back is also bruised. We have to put a stop to this violence!"

"I agree! Do you want me to go to school with you?"

"Yes. I think that may be necessary."

The next day, they were in the school office an hour before the first bell to see the principal. They were shown to his office immediately.

"Sir, look at my son's hands. The bleeding has stopped, but his hands are still bruised. His teacher hit him because he was writing with his left hand!"

"Mrs. Ballard, are you sure that was the only reason she hit him? Teachers shouldn't hit students. Is there any chance that Rex was being violent or disruptive?"

"Look at his file! Does he have any record of violence or unacceptable behavior?"

It took about 2 minutes for his secretary to bring in the file.

"Looking at this file, it seems he has been to the nurse's office several times. Rex must be very clumsy?"

"Clumsy! Are you kidding me? Rex gets assaulted by the boys in his class at least twice a day. They kick him and punch him. He sees the nurse when his asthma gets so bad that he can't breathe! Do you know how hard it is to explain to an emergency room doctor that you didn't cause the bruises? That every boy in his class bullied your child! The only reason the doctor believes us is because Rex can provide the names of each boy involved."

"Well Mrs. Ballard, boys will be boys. It's natural for them to fight when they are playing."

It was Tom who went off this time. "Is it PLAYING when my son has to spend 2 weeks in the hospital because his bloodwork shows organ damage? Is it PLAYING when he can't even breathe without help when he arrives?"

Principal Holmes stopped short. "No, I don't suppose it is. We can't watch every boy during their outdoors time. The attraction of this school is that we have fields and a park where the kids can play. But each class only has one teacher to watch the class. The teachers have to watch the girls because they are more likely to get hurt on the playground equipment."

"What are we supposed to do? Wait for the boys to just kill him?"

"No. We'll have to work out something. I'll talk to his teachers about that."

"What about this teacher who is beating my son with a ruler? Isn't that against the rules?"

"Yes. It violates school policy and state laws. She came from a parochial school where they allow corporal punishment. Why was she hitting him again?"

"Because he was writing with his left hand!"

"Why does he write with his left hand?"

"Rex is left-handed. He eats, sews, knits, and crochets left handed. When he was about to start kindergarten, he got his finger caught in a swing-set and it nearly chopped off the middle finger on his right hand. They reattached it, but it took almost a year for the muscles and nerves to heal."

"Oh! I see! I'll talk to her immediately. I would prefer to do this myself. Having you and Rex present would limit my ability to address this issue fully."

Miss Johnston never used a ruler on any of her students again. Rex could write with his left hand.

Mrs. Gifford tried to watch the boys a little more carefully. She had learned to spot the assaults. By the time she blew the whistle, and the boys broke up, Rex was already hurt. Only Rex seemed knew who did what.

Attempts to punish the most obvious of the bullies proved impossible. Several of the boys had fathers who were lawyers. The PTA closely connected the other parents. Many on the PTA still wanted Rex expelled.

Meanwhile, Rex was practically home-schooled. He was in the hospital so often and for so long that he was doing more schoolwork in the hospital than at school. Often, when he got back to school, he was weeks ahead of the other classes.

4H AND HOBBIES

Rex joined 4H club. It thrilled him when he found he was one of 2 boys among 8 girls in the leather craft group, and one of 2 boys and 6 girls in the photography group.

One of Rex's friends from the 4H leather group was Eddie Wolf.

The boys who bullied him had regularly used the phrase "aussie wassiee I'm a Nazi", often before attacking.

When Rex was at Eddie's house, he used that phrase, not really having a clue what it meant.

"You're a Nazi, eh?" It was Eddie's grandmother.

She grabbed Rex's arm to make him look at her arm. She pulled up her sleeve. There were numbers branded onto her arm.

"THAT'S what the NAZIS did to us! Most of us had tattoos, but we kept changing the numbers so they wouldn't kill us. To make it harder, they branded the numbers into our arms. To stay out of the gas chambers, we had to burn the changes to the numbers, all without making noise."

Rex cried. "That's so terrible! I didn't even know what that phrase meant. It still makes no sense to me."

Eddie's mom come over. "It's OK Rex. You didn't know. Several of the kids at school are the children of Nazis who escaped from Germany after World War Two. Mostly scientists and doctors. Others, like us, were survivors of the camps."

"I need to get a library book so I can read more about that. I'll talk to my parents too."

Rex went home. His mother told him about the Nazi concentration camps. Tom helped him find a history book in the adult section that he could read. None of the young adult books even mentioned the death camps.

CHEMISTRY AND SCIENCE

For Christmas, Rex got a chemistry set. He had wanted a Barbie, but he had been reading a few books on chemistry. This was a way to learn more.

Rex and Tom used the set together until Tom realized he could trust Rex not to poison himself. He was very good at following the procedures listed for each experiment.

Tom and Rex even made explosives with his chemistry set. They made gunpowder, nitroglycerin, and incendiaries. They only made small quantities, carefully, and they neutralized the experiments when done.

They had fun putting a few drops of nitro between two washers held in place by nuts on a bolt. When they threw them on the ground, they were like large firecrackers.

Rex learned how to make chloroform. For a few days, he used it to help him fall asleep. He had been only getting 2 or 3 hours of sleep every night. The chloroform put him to sleep for almost 6 hours. It gave him headaches, so he stopped using it.

MAGIC AND PRAYER

Rex looked for any method of changing his sex. He even found a few books on black magic in the adult section. He couldn't find anything about how to change sex or exchange bodies with a girl.

Rex couldn't find stories or science or even medical journals on sex change or boys who wanted to be girls. There were episodes on Gilligan's Isle, Star Trek, The Munster's, and other television shows where boys and girls changed bodies or boys became girls. He realized that was just fantasy.

Rex had learned that there was no Santa Claus by the time he was three. He shattered his belief in tooth fairies and Easter Bunnies by first grade. Was it all a lie? Wishes never came true! Especially his one deepest wish! Yet Rex still believed in God. He thought there were limitations, even to God.

Rex had also learned how to build and fly model airplanes. Tom helped him build a "chug" coaster. He gave up riding it after some boys tried to steal it. They beat him up again, too.

CARIH—ASTHMA STUDY

The insurance company told Rex's parents that there was a research project to study kids with asthma. They practically insisted that they go. They offered to pay all expenses, including mileage and related costs.

Every night, Rex would immediately after school after school. Lois would drive 30 minutes across town. Rex would get a physical exam, including blood pressure, heart rate, and lung capacity, and other tests.

Next, there would be a form with several questions about how the day went, how the patient felt, what moods did they experience, and to what level of intensity? After that, there would be time with a psychiatrist who would ask a few questions based on the form to find out why there were stronger emotions.

This continued for 13 weeks. Rex was also open about telling how many times the boys had attacked him and how often.

At the end of the first phase, they decided Rex qualified for "Phase 2" research. Rex's family stayed in a pleasant hotel while Rex lived with Joanne. Joanne was the housemother for the girl's dorm. This phase of the trial was to last 8 weeks. Rex would continue to come in after school for the daily evaluations, then he would spend a few hours with Joanne in the girls' dorm.

Something remarkable happened. On the first few days, Rex left school coughing so hard he was choking. Every breath was a loud and audible wheeze. However, when Joanne and Rex went to the girls' dorm, Rex calmed down. He made friends with several of the girls almost immediately.

Each night, his asthma got better. Joanne and Rex had to go to the girl's dorm all day Saturday, and Rex would join the girls in time for American Band Stand. With a little encouragement from the other girls, Rex was soon doing the popular dances. The Twist, the Swim, the Boogaloo, the "Go Go", and a few others that didn't have names. Rex would smile and giggle with the rest of the girls. By the end of the day, he was singing along with the radio. He wasn't even wheezing anymore.

By the end of the 8 weeks, Rex had invited the girls over for a party. They cooked and cleaned up together. They had fun all day long. Not only did none of the other girls have asthma, but Rex didn't show any sign of asthma either. Rex's health improved radically. His lung capacity, blood pressure, and heart were improving.

By the end of this phase, Rex could go through an entire meal without even clearing his throat. He hadn't needed an inhaler for almost 3 weeks. During the psychological profiles, Rex was much calmer, much happier, cried less, and got angry less. He even elaborated on how much he enjoyed being with the other girls.

There was another 6 weeks when Rex's family came back. Rex's health quickly went downhill. Rex wheezed again. He needed inhaler and medication every day. Some of this may have been related to the fact that both of Rex's parents were chain smokers at home. Rex would often come home to a cloud in the family room.

When the sun came in on the smoke-filled room, Rex would have to ask, "Mom, are you there?" She would respond from her sewing machine in the corner of the room only 8 feet away. Rex was looking right at her and couldn't see her.

The people at CARIH wondered if Rex should move into the dorms. They had Rex stay with Sylvia, the boy's housemother, for 8 weeks, to see if he could adapt. Things didn't go well at all.

After the exams, Rex and Sylvia would go to the boys' dorm, and Rex would try to play with the boys. He would barely talk. He seemed to be afraid of everyone, and when a boy got angry, Rex would back away as far and fast as he could.

Rex's health got much worse. Even with no cigarettes anywhere, Rex's asthma got so bad that he almost had to be hospitalized. Even Rex's color was blue. And the daily tests and surveys showed he was getting upset all the time, crying a lot, having temper tantrums, and was almost never happy.

It was almost as if he was under as much stress as he could stand. His lung capacity and function were dropping dangerously low. They almost had to stop the test.

When Rex got back with his parents, his health improved, but was still very poor. This contradicted the theory that it was ONLY the smoking. They confirmed that the severity of the Asthma was directly related to the severity of the negative emotions and lack of positive ones.

Miss Johnston asked Lois to come in and meet. There was an issue that she needed to talk about personally.

"Mrs. Ballard, I don't know how to tell you this, but I'm afraid that Rex might be mentally retarded."

"That makes no sense! He reads at high school level already and seems very intelligent."

"I don't know what to tell you. His raw score was 65. He may need to go into a special program."

Two weeks later, Lois got a call from Principal Holmes. "Could you please come in? I need to talk to you face to face."

"Principal Holmes, I know you're going to tell me Rex is retarded and needs to be put in a Special Ed program. I don't see how it's possible. Rex isn't retarded!"

"Your Right Mrs. Ballard. Rex isn't retarded."

"What?! But the IQ test?"

"It's true. His raw score is low. It turned out that he answered every question in order, including questions that no one his age should have been able to understand, let alone get right. Rex got every single one right. He only answered two-thirds of the questions, but all his answers were correct. He may be a genius. Can you get him a verbal IQ test?"

That night, at their visit to CARIH, Lois asked Dr. Purcell if they could do the verbal IQ test. They set it up for the following day.

Rex surprised the woman administering the test. He answered nearly every question correctly. One was particularly interesting. "What is Chile?"

"Chilly, that's a temperature between 33 Fahrenheit, above freezing, and below 60, a low room temperature."

She realized he had correctly described the homonym and provided 2 additional supporting facts. "Can you think of another kind of Chile?"

"Yes Chili, really great food. I make mine with pinto beans, kidney beans, ground beef, then I add chili powder, salt, Tabasco sauce, and cinnamon. Mom just uses the seasoning pouch."

Rex had provided another correct answer for another homonym, given the verbal test.

"Can you think of a place?"

"Oh yeah! Chile, the country on the western coast of South America, below Brazil, north of Tierra del Fuego!"

"Tierra del Fuego?"

"Yes, at the southern tip. The natives saw the southern Aurora and thought it was fire. So, they called it the Land of Fire."

How would she score this? As 3 correct answers plus a geography lesson?

Then she said, "Now we are going to do a different test. I'm going to show you some pictures of some people. I want you to tell me how they feel."

"She's sad."

"He's mad."

"She's pretending to be happy, but she's nervous."

"He's up to mischief. I think he's happy about it."

They continued through 20 more pictures.

"Now I'm going to show you some drawings. I want you to tell me what's going on."

"The mommy tiger is fixing dinner. The daddy lion is reading the newspaper. I think he's upset about a story he's reading. He's smoking a pipe to relax. The two kids, the kittens, are playing a game of jacks. They are really having fun."

They continued through 20 more of those pictures.

"Now I'm going to show you some pictures. I want you to tell me what you would like to do if you were in that picture."

"Oh, she's cold, and she's alone. I'd like to give her a blanket and be her friend. We could even share the blanket together. Maybe mom would even let her keep it."

"The boys are playing softball or baseball. I don't really like to play, but I might chase the balls they hit too far. If I chase it, it's a home run."

"The lady is cooking. I'd offer to chop the vegetables, or peel potatoes, depending on what she's cooking."

They went through twenty pictures.

"OK Rex, I'm going to take you to a playroom while I talk to you mom, dad, and Dr. Purcell."

"May I please just sit at a desk and draw or write? That would be more fun for me, if it's OK?".

"That would be fine. You can wait here."

The adults then went into Dr. Purcell's office.

"I've seen nothing like this!"

"What do you mean?"

"Dr. Purcell, I gave Rex the verbal IQ test which measures intellectual intelligence, but I also gave him a test of emotional intelligence. Most kids with exceptionally high IQs are sociopaths. They don't have high emotional intelligence. Normally, girls score higher on the emotional intelligence, but about average on intellect. Rex aced both tests!"

This relieved Lois. "So, he's not retarded?"

Dr. Purcell looked at the notes and the scores and started laughing. "No Mrs. Ballard, your son is not only an intellectual Genius, but an emotional Genius as well. He scored over 180 on each test."

Tom sighed. "That's a relief. What do we tell the school?"

"I'll send a note with his scores on both tests. However, Rex's scores are so high, I want to give him the Mensa test in about 3 days. The schools and if officially recognized their test. If I'm right, he can join Mensa and have his score officially recorded."

After Rex took the Mensa test, which was untimed, Dr. Purcell looked at the answers, scored them, and sent in the test, which included not only the answers but also Rex's notes on how he arrived at his answers.

"It looks like Rex's IQ is close to 190. I must send it in to Mensa to get the official score. Sometimes the notes can lead to a higher or lower score. I'll have the official results in a week."

A week later, Dr. Purcell sat down with Tom and Lois while Rex waited in another room.

"Congratulations! Your is officially a genius! He provided 3 original correct answers. It's unusually to provide even one. He has an official IQ of 195. I am giving you a copy for the school. It will cost you $200 for him to join Mensa, but it will open some doors. He could even go to a special school for gifted children."

Tom winced. "Didn't Ricky go to one? He seems to be a bully now."

Lois nodded. "Yes. Marion was so proud when Rick went to that school for gifted students. Rick got smarter, but he got meaner too."

"I'm sorry, Dr. Purcell. I can't afford to spend $200 for some honorary club for snobs. If we have the official score, that will be good enough."

"That's fine. This score is good for up to two years. After that he would have to retake the Mensa test to join."

"I just worry that Rex would be worse off in a school full of kids like Rick. He's so sensitive."

"Remember that Emotional Intelligence score we talked about last week? Rex's emotional intelligence is so high it's almost like he can read people's minds. Unfortunately, he is better at seeing anger, fear, and pain because these are stronger emotions. It's highly unlikely that Rex would become a sociopath."

The results qualified Rex for phase 4 research. Rex would see a psychologist every day, and the visits would gradually decrease. Rex came in to see Dr Rennie every day. At first, they just tried to talk, but Rex didn't seem to communicate very well. He would answer direct questions, and talk briefly about that day's assaults, but didn't open up.

One day, Rex brought a Morse code key set, and sent "I want to be a girl" over the short wires. Rex was under the desk when he sent the message. Dr Rennie was decoding from above his desk. When Dr Rennie saw the message, he said, "Do you really want to be a girl?". Rex nodded and broke into tears.

What happened next shocked Rex!

Dr Rennie said, "We KNOW you want to be a girl. You probably should have BEEN a girl, but we can't change what you are now. We can't talk about this anymore because something terrible could happen if we did. I will help you cope with the boys so that you don't get hurt so much. Would that be OK?"

Rex was so obviously disappointed he almost wanted to stop everything right then. He slowly nodded his head like he was accepting his punishment, life in prison without the possibility of parole.

Dr Rennie would ask about the things the boys did. The stories were terrible. A few times, Dr Rennie asked Rex to lift his shirt so he could see how many bruises there were. Some days, black-and-blue almost covered his back and stomach. He would ask what the boys said, and he would ask how Rex reacted.

When the boys threatened him, Rex would cry or try to run away. This would cause the boys to chase him and beat him up. Even how he walked was being affected. Dr Rennie knew from a recent chest X-ray that something damaged Rex's spine in several places, but not enough to justify surgery.

SPOCK

Dr Rennie started playing role play games. He would pretend to be the boys who bullied Rex. Rex had to control his emotions. Rex remembered Spock, the Vulcan on Star Trek. He didn't watch it that much because he liked Time Tunnel better. Spock became a new role model.

Later, Rex had to make Dr Rennie laugh after he hurled the insults.

Rex learned how to HELP the boys make fun of him. Rex almost walked like a duck because his feet went out and he had large hips and curvature of the spine that made his butt look far too big for a boy.

When the boys would tease him for walking like a duck, he would exaggerate the walk and start quacking. Rex even learned how to sound like Donald Duck, talking out through one of his cheeks. The bullying became less frequent and less severe, but didn't stop entirely.

Rex kept bringing up his desire to be a girl, but Dr Rennie tried to talk him out of it.

"You would have to get shots every day!"

"Ok, I already get allergy shots."

"You would have to have surgery. That would be painful."

"More painful than the boys beating me up every day?"

"You would have to do housework."

"I already do most of the housework, and I enjoy doing it."

"Your family would have to move."

"Or I could go to the other school that's only about 3 blocks further to walk."

Clearly, Rex had been willing to go to great lengths to become a girl.

The doctor called for a private consultation with his parents.

"We have a problem. Rex wants to become a girl."

Lois nodded. "I knew he does, but is that possible?"

"In theory, yes. Psychologically, he is a girl. He thrives when he plays with girls. He is happiest when he plays with girls. If it were practical and legal, I'd say that was the best course. Unfortunately, it's not practical."

Lois put her hand down. "Rex barely survived 30 hospitalizations, and he's still getting beat up. What would it take for him to be a girl?"

"First, Rex would have to be injected with hormones regularly. It would be much like his allergy shots. Second, he would have to be castrated, preferably before puberty. Finally, he would need corrective surgery to create a vagina. It's all painful and expensive."

Tom sat straight. "How expensive!"

"The entire process could cost as much as $100,000, but not all at once."

Tom went into shock. "That's over four times as much as our house is worth. There's no way I could afford that."

"Then we have another problem."

Lois was struggling with how easily the men had dismissed the prospect of Rex at least living as a girl in school.

"What's the problem Doctor!"

"I had them do a blood test during one of his weekly physical exams. Rex's testosterone level is unusually low, even for a boy his age. His estrogen levels are much higher than a normal boy."

Tom smirked. "Rex has no nuts. They're undescended. They'll come down when he gets older, right?"

Dr Rennie shook his head.

"I think Rex will need testosterone shots. There is no way he would agree to them. We'll have to tell him they are allergy shots. This may help him have a normal male puberty."

SPINAL SNAP

One day, Rex had done dreadful at softball, and the team wanted to beat him up. Rex tried to run away and headed for a tree so that he could climb up out of reach. This would at least give him time until the bell rang.

Unfortunately, as he was swinging up, one boy grabbed his legs and began pulling them behind so that Rex's stomach was facing the ground. One of the other boys started tickling him. When Rex let go of the tree, the boy holding his feet still had them about 4 feet above the ground.

Rex hit the ground on his chest and shoulders. He tried to breathe, but he couldn't. There was incredible pain between his shoulders, radiating from his spine. He couldn't move his legs, either. One boy tried to kick him and Rex didn't even flinch, because he COULDN'T.

Suddenly one boy said, "He can't breathe, get Mrs. Gifford!".

By the time Mrs. Gifford finally came, Rex was nearly unconscious. His face and arms were a dark blue. It had been nearly 4 minutes, and Rex STILL hadn't taken a breath.

One boy said, "He's not breathing!"

Only his head was moving. There was no time to do anything safe. Mrs. Gifford was out of time. She picked him up, crossed his arms in front of him, put her arms around his shoulders and folded arms, and jumped. Instantly, Rex started breathing again. He was too weak to stand, so the teacher carried him back to the nurse.

The next day, the doctor took an x-ray. "You are lucky to be alive! It almost looks like they broke your spine, right at the shoulder blades. I won't touch your back because it might kill you. It's another miracle."

After that, Rex didn't have to play with the boys anymore. He brought a butterfly net and chased butterflies and grasshoppers. Sometimes he would pretend that a grasshopper was a boy who bullied him. He would stick it in an anthill, watching the little ants slowly tear it apart. Rex talked about that with Dr Rennie, who asked if Rex wanted to do terrible things to the real boy. Rex shook his head and said "No, I just want him to stay away from me".

There was another girl in Rex's class. Her name was Melody. She was a nice girl, but much taller and stronger than the other girls. She was almost more like a boy. When the boys picked on her, she would grab them and hit them.

The boys called her "IT". Not a boy, not a girl, not even human, just "IT". Rex felt sorry for Melody and tried to be nice to her. Soon, they were close friends. She was bossy. Rex didn't mind. He was just happy to have her as a friend. Rex decided he was an "IT" too, and proud of it.

Rex had a few other friends. They didn't want anybody to know they were friends. Eventually, Rex understood they were afraid of getting beat up. Rex protected their secret, not calling them friends while at school. Rex even made friends with a few of the new kids. He warned them they had to keep their friendship a secret so that they wouldn't get hurt.

SEX EDUCATION—SORT OF

When Rex was 10, Lois had walked in on Rex unexpectedly. He was wearing her boots, a skirt, a blouse, and her wig. And vacuuming the floor.

A few months earlier, Lois got a haircut and said she needed a wig because she hated the way her hair looked. Dad took her out, and they got one that was darker than her natural hair, more like the color of Rex's hair. Then she stopped wearing it because it was uncomfortable.

That winter, she had bought some boots for winter. They had to be two sizes too big to fit over her swollen ankle. She hated them and stopped wearing them by February.

At first, Lois thought Rex had brought a girl home with him, but this girl was vacuuming the floor. Then Rex turned, panicked, and locked the doors to his room while changed out of the clothes. Lois didn't want to talk about it, but she talked to Tom about it that night.

Tom decided Rex needed to know about the "Birds and the Bees". He started reading several books to Rex. Books on gender, male parts, and female parts, how they would change. At one point, Rex said "I have a tiny penis, but I don't have testes. Why is that?"

This was the awkward issue that Tom had tried to avoid confronting. Tom drew a picture of a body. He drew a little penis between the legs.

Then he said, "Most boys have testicles down here", pointing to the right and left of the penis. Then he drew to little circles up inside the body about halfway between the penis and the belly button on each side of the penis.

He said, "Your testicles are still up inside you, like ovaries. If they don't come down by the time you are 12, the doctor will have to perform surgery."

Rex said with a big eager smile, "You mean I'm like a GIRL and just have a little penis?".

Tom looked almost sad. "Almost, but you have testicles rather than ovaries. They are just in the wrong place."

In that one phrase, Rex's expression went from overjoyed with hope, to despondent, almost ready to cry.

Rex slumped. "I don't want to be a man! I don't want to know any more about sex!".

Tom knew Rex needed testosterone shots. They would have to make sure Rex didn't know what they were. The Doctor agreed to call them "Allergy shots", so that Rex wouldn't refuse them.

GAY?

The next day, Tom told Rex to go into the bedroom with him. He closed the door behind them and he pulled out a copy of Playboy Magazine. He opened the magazine to a picture of a naked girl.

"This is what a naked girl looks like."

Rex seemed unimpressed.

Rex looked at her face. "She has pretty eyes. I like her makeup!"

There was no sign of arousal or interest.

That night, Tom told Lois, "I think Rex might be a homosexual. He doesn't seem sexually attracted to girls at all."

Lois knew Rex had been trying on her clothes. She even found panty hose, a slip, and a teddy hidden between the box spring and the mattress.

"Find some pictures of girls in sexy lingerie, see how he reacts to that."

About 2 days later, Tom pulled Rex into the parent's bedroom, and showed him a copy of Penthouse. He opened it to a picture of a girl wearing black silk stockings, silky panties, a garter belt, and a sheer bra.

Rex grabbed the magazine. All he could think about was how much he wanted to wear those pretty clothes. He thought about how nice it would feel. Repeatedly turning back to the page with the girl still fully clothed. He wanted to BE the girl I that picture. Being that girl and being with that girl at the same time was something he always imagined. It aroused him and Tom could see his interest, but not his thinking.

Then his father flipped to another page with a man and a woman together. Rex looked at the man and said, "That's gross, his penis is huge, and his testicles are just ugly". Rex wasn't gay.

To Rex, anything related to boys was something to be avoided, a threat. There was ZERO desire to even think about taking a chance that the guy might try to hurt him. Pleasure was the last thing on Rex's mind when he saw ANY picture of a man not wearing a suit.

Rex liked his dad, and he liked his grandfather, but there were very few others. Doctors gave him shots, dentists hurt his mouth, and boys would hit him and kick him. Even after the beatings ended, the fear had been so embedded, so traumatic, that the fear continued to dominate his thinking about boys and men.

For as long as Rex could remember, his romantic story book ending was him as a beautiful princess like Sleeping Beauty or Snow White being kissed by a beautiful princess instead of a prince.

He liked to think about being a beautiful girl in a sexy dress or skirt suit, being kissed by another girl who wanted to kiss him. He would imagine himself as Susan Day from Partridge Family being seduced by Honey West, Joey Heatherton, or Anne Margret.

TEEN IDOLS

Rex spent a lot of time with two girls from his church named Debbie and Sandy. They would listen to music together, play Barbies, and enjoy "girl talk" together.

Debbie liked Mickey Dolenz of the Monkees and David Cassidy on the Partridge Family.

Sandy liked Peter Tork.

Rex thought David Cassidy and Davy Jones from the Monkees were cute. Maybe because they seemed harmless. They might be nice to him if he were a girl.

Rex watched the shows and talked with Debbie & Sandy about them. They imagined being kissed and hugged by them, but with him as a girl. He found he liked the idea. He struggled with the idea of a boy kissing him like a boy. That didn't appeal to Rex at all.

From the time he was about four, he would have nightmares. They would start the same, with him as a pretty girl in a blue dress with petticoats and a full skirt, sitting on the lap of her boyfriend with his legs between hers. She seemed happy. Then somebody hit her boyfriend, knocking him out, and an older man put something around her neck and strangled her.

As she "fell asleep", Rex would wake up trying to figure out why she was in this little boy's body. It was a recurring nightmare. It seemed so real, in color, with lots of details. Could this nightmare be memories of the last moments of a previous life?

THE REVELATION

Lois had discovered Rex's secret stash of clothes buried under a pile of coats in a bag in the back corner of his closet. She found underwear, a skirt, and a shiny satin blouse, as well as a nightie and a teddy. She confronted Rex about it.

The next day, Lois met Rex on the way into his bedroom. He was looking in the closet.

Lois held a bag in her hand. "Looking for these?"

It was the bag where he hid his girl's clothes in the back of the closet.

"You STOLE one of my teddies without asking."

Rex started crying.

"I wish I WAS a girl! Sorry for stealing. I wish I didn't have to steal and hide!"

Rex hated being called a thief.

"I hate stealing and sneaking! But how am I going to get girl clothes? Dad sure won't buy them for me! I can't afford them with my quarter a week allowance!"

Lois paused, stunned at the response. Rex had a point.

"I don't mind if you take from the goodwill bag or the knotted hose, but I don't like you stealing things out of my drawers. I don't mind your dressing up when no one is home, but I DO mind you're stealing!"

Rex apologized and offered to give the teddy back. He'd worn it a LOT, and it showed. Some ruffles had even come off.

Lois calmed down. "It's OK. I hated that teddy anyway. You should ask instead of stealing. You are stealing my clothes and I don't like it. I hated that teddy, so you can keep it. But stop stealing. I don't want you to be a thief." Rex looked like he had just been told his dog died.

Lois could see the life draining. The smile disappeared. Instead, he was silent, numb, like he was dead inside.

He walked into his bedroom, shut the door. Lois could hear him murmur "I just wanna die."

Lois thought for a moment. Rex had first told her he wanted to be a girl when he was six, and at CARIH, when he stayed with the girls, he was so healthy and so happy. Could it be that Rex was a girl inside? Was that even possible?

Lois went through some old mementos. She remembered something unusual about the little birth certificate they used to label the bassinet. When she found it in an envelope, she pulled it out, and there it was. The label read "Clark Boy?". Lois couldn't believe her eyes. Why would there be a question mark? That night, she talked to Tom about it.

The kids had gone to bed before Lois was alone with Tom. She was getting more and more determined to find out what was going on.

Lois pulled out the label. "Tom, what is this about? Why was there a question mark on Rex's bassinet when he was born?"

Tom sighed. "When Rex was born, you had been through a hell of a labor. You had been in labor for at least 48 hours, and that didn't include the two-hour drive from Fort Collins to Denver. You were exhausted. They had knocked you out so you could get some needed rest. They worried you might go critical if you didn't get some sleep."

Lois looked very confused. "What does THAT have to do with the question mark on Rex's bassinet?".

"When they came out to tell me Rex had been born, they told me there was a problem. He had some unusual things going on down there. They weren't sure whether he was a boy or a girl. He had a penis, but it was unusually small. You've probably noticed that."

Lois nodded. "Yes. I didn't really notice until Walt was born, but you're right, Rex is much smaller, almost a quarter as big as Walt."

Tom leaned forward; "You've also noticed that Rex didn't have testicles when he was born, or even as a boy?"

Lois nodded slowly; "Yes, but the doctor told us they just hadn't come down."

Tom sighed, rolled his eyes, and looked straight into Lois's beautiful brown eyes, and said, "That night, there were other problems too. Rex had a small penis, but he also didn't have a sack. He had lips."

Lois squinted, unable to believe her ears. "You mean vaginal lips?".

Tom winced, "Exactly! The doctor said that gender ambiguity was not that rare, but that this was a more unusual case. Rex had some boy parts and girl parts."

Lois couldn't believe what she was hearing. "You mean our son is really our daughter?"

Tom nodded; "Sort of like that. He was a bit of both. They could make him one or the other or leave him the way he was."

Lois looked at Tom with a sidelong glance. "So you made him a boy?"

Tom nodded, expecting Lois to explode any second.

"The doctor told me he could turn her into a girl, or turn him into a boy. There was no way to tell for sure what was inside without a dangerous exploratory surgery. He said that it would be easier to turn the boy into a girl later, but almost impossible to turn the girl into a boy if I made that decision."

Tom pleaded, "I wanted to talk to you first, but the doctor told me it needed to be done immediately, because once there was an official record one way or the other, they couldn't change it as easily. He recommended we go for a boy. I hope I got it right, but I'm not sure. Those cortisone shots he was getting as a baby also included testosterone to normalize him as a boy."

Lois met Rex as he came home after school. She said, "Since you've been doing the laundry anyway, nobody but us has to know. If I tie stockings or pantyhose, you can wash them and keep them. If I put anything in the goodwill bag, you can keep them, too. That way, you won't steal clothes I still want to wear."

PERIODS?

A few weeks later, something unusual happened. One night, Rex was trying to go to the bathroom. He started having these terrible cramps. It almost felt like someone had kicked him between the legs, but they were long and painful. The cramps had been getting worse for a few days. He was in so much pain he started crying, even screaming in pain.

When his parents woke up, Lois gave him a laxative and a Darvon. She used them to relieve her menstrual cramps. About 2 hours later, the Darvon had kicked in, and Rex could push out this big "plug" about 3 inches in diameter and 4 inches long.

Then came a flood, like his insides were draining. Rex wiped himself off and stood up. He investigated the bowl and realized that the liquid was a dark red. Rex thought he had hurt something, so he called in his parents.

Lois saw it and said, "Oh my God, that's blood".

Tom told her everything was fine, but she should take Rex to the doctor in the morning.

The doctor did a preliminary exam and then told Rex to wait in the waiting room. "Lois, I don't know what's wrong at the moment. You described blood that sounds like internal bleeding. It seems like the bleeding has stopped for now. If it happens again, I want you to mark it on the calendar and call me, even if it's late at night. These may be periods."

SHOPPING

A few minutes later, Lois came out with a look of shock on her face. She hugged Rex as he stood up.

"Let's go shopping."

Lois went clothes shopping at Lerner's and asked Rex what clothes he liked best. Rex picked out modern styles, shorter skirts, and pretty blouses, with satin or lace or ruffles. They almost seemed too large for Lois, but she bought them anyway.

Lois wore the outfit that Rex chose to their church. She got dozens of compliments. People loved her look and told her she looked great. Lois loved getting the compliments. She realized Rex had a good sense of fashion.

Rex did the laundry. He folded the clothes and put them away, and the next day found the blouse and skirt in the "Goodwill" pile, which meant Rex could take them, no questions asked.

SHE also noticed that his mom had tied the knot in two pairs of good pantyhose. Lois tied the knot when the hose had a run. Rex washed them, then he could throw them away or keep them. These were not run and wearable.

The next day, while Lois was at work, Rex got dressed up in the new blouse, skirt, and a pair of underwear he had rescued from the goodwill pile. Then he pulled on the boots. To his amazement, they fit. Then he put on his mom's brunette wig. What he saw in the mirror was the beautiful girl he had always wanted to be. He even put on some make-up, including blush, mascara, and lipstick.

Rex liked his outfit so much he wore it all afternoon. His brother and sister were down the block playing with friends.

Rex did the laundry, vacuuming, and dusting, as well as making the beds. It was so much more fun when he did it as a girl. He put his boy clothes in the hamper just in case the kids came home early.

Rex almost lost track of time. He finished all his chores. He was doing some cooking, chopping up some veggies when he heard the voice of his sister and one of her friends.

Rex ran to the bathroom, locked the bathroom door, and scrambled to get out of the clothes as fast as he could. He even hid the wig in the hamper. There were several such "Close Calls", not to mention a few unexpected visits from Lois who would drop in for lunch, come home early, or pick up something she forgot.

She came home while Rex was vacuuming. She saw Rex in the skirt, blouse, wig, and boots, cheerfully vacuuming the floor.

Lois just stood there and watched. When Rex turned off the vacuum, Lois said, "Rex?"

Rex turned around. The sight stunned Lois. What she saw was a beautiful young girl. She was as pretty as any girl in his school or church. In fact, she was beautiful. She had noticed that Rex seemed more graceful and at ease. She couldn't believe her eyes.

Rex ran into his bedroom, locked the doors, and stripped everything off and changed into his boy clothes. He came back out looking like she had grounded him for a week. Like he did when he had done something terrible.

Lois looked at him. She didn't know what to say. She came over and gave him a hug.

If Rex didn't want to talk, she didn't want to force the issue. He seemed so afraid and so ashamed when 'she' ran away.

Lois feared she might do more harm than good. She couldn't bear to tell him he couldn't be a girl.

Rex desperately wanted to talk, more than ever. He was coming apart inside. She yearned to tell her mom again how much she wanted to be a girl. She wanted to be her daughter.

The girl inside was screaming to come out and LIVE! She wanted to go out and play. She wanted friends and family who loved, accepted, and acknowledged her.

What SHE didn't want was to be shot down or ignored yet again. She had tried so many times to tell her parents who and what she was, and they shut her down each time.

Rex misinterpreted his mother's silence as rejection. She didn't even want to acknowledge the girl inside. The girl wanted to scream, to cry, to do anything to be recognized. Instead, there was silence and denial.

That night, Rex asked his mom, "If I had been a girl, what would you have named me?".

Lois hoped that this might be the opening. "I liked Louise. Your dad's mom's name was Gladys, your aunt got named Ernestine after your grandfather, but we called her Suzy because she hated it so much."

Rex wrinkled his face. "So, they would have called me Lou? Or worse?".

Mom said, "your grandmother's name was Fern, and her mother's name was Eunice, but I didn't like those either." The conversation was over. Silence. Rex walked away. She had lost her chance to talk.

After a few weeks, Rex ventured outside for short walks. He looked like a girl, and in the boots, with their 2-inch heels, he even walked like a girl. Much more gracefully than usual.

During the summer, Walt and Diane were down the street playing with friends. The last thing they wanted to do was help Rex with housework, so Rex had the house all to himself.

Rex spent most of the summer dressed as a girl, looking and acting very much like a housewife. Before his mother came home, he tried to get back into boy mode. Rex dreaded that if she caught him, she would take away all his girl clothes and make him go back to being a boy all the time.

For the first time in a long time, Rex was happy, and it showed in his health. He hadn't had a single asthma attack in over six months, and Dr. Rennie was ready to declare the research a smashing success. Rex would be one of the featured cases when they wrote the study up.

Lois seemed to be much happier and was really enjoying her job. That summer, something miraculous happened. Neither Rex nor Lois had been to the hospital in over 6 months.

SAVED

Lois and Tom started talking to Rex about Jesus. Of course, by this time, Rex knew about Jesus. He had read the bible several times. His grandfather had read him all 4 gospels at least a dozen times.

Now his parents were asking. "Do you want to have a personal relationship with Jesus? Do you want Jesus to be part of your life?"

Rex nodded. "I've always wanted him to be part of my life. I know he helps me, but what are you talking about?"

Rex had a conflict. God had pulled him through asthma attacks, assaults, and medical treatments. But God had still failed to give him the ability to be a girl. Was this the missing ingredient?

"Do you want to be saved? Do you want to be baptized with the Holy Spirit?"

Rex knew the stories about Peter and the Apostles being baptized and preaching in everybody's language.

Lois said, "You are old enough to make that decision for yourself, but it has to be your decision."

Rex was direct. "Of course, I want to be saved."

So together they said the prayer. Rex got saved.

Tom and Lois took Rex to a group of Pentecostal Christians. They performed miracle healing, and many other things. They performed many miracles. Rex continued to go to the meetings through the summer.

Rex asked God again the prayer that he had prayed thousands of times.

"God, if you want me to be a boy, help me be happy being a boy! If you want me to be a girl, help me become a girl!"

It was the prayer that was never answered. Could God want him to be stuck in this limbo between boy and girl? How could God use that to his advantage?

Rex had been wishing, praying, and hoping to be a girl. He wished on the first star of the night, on the shooting stars he saw in the mountains, on 4 leaf clovers, when he won the winning part of the drumstick, and blowing out the candles on birthday cakes.

He had even looked up books on spiritual magic. Rex found a few library books on black magic. He read the stories about Don Giovanni, Don Juan, and Faust.

There was one very dark spell that involved poisoning a child to force their soul out, then killing yourself so your soul could go into the child's body. In theory, the poison would wear off and the child would awaken with your soul in it. But there didn't seem to be much proof that the spell worked.

The thought that he could sell his soul to the devil and become a girl tempted Rex, but he realized such things had a horrible cost. He'd already seen enough "previews of hell" to decide that this was not an option. If God didn't want to make him a boy, or a girl, Rex could not risk selling his soul.

Rex didn't realize that Don Giovani was a story of a castrato, a boy who asked to be castrated, sang soprano, and became a legendary "lover", seducing many women while playing one on stage.

DEATH'S DOOR

The first day of school turned out to be a trip to the hospital.

Rex eagerly hopped out of bed and crumbled like wet paper. He ended up on the floor, and he couldn't get up.

He started puking and a few seconds later had filled his underwear and much of the floor. Lois came in, trying to get him to hurry, only to see him lying on his side on the floor, in the mess.

He couldn't even talk. "Mom, I can't move. Help me get up or they might not put me in Mr. Donald's class."

She felt his head, "My God, you are burning up!"

She went and got a thermometer, and a pot for him to puke in. When she pulled out the thermometer, it read 105 degrees.

She called the doctor, who told her, "Get to the emergency room at Children's Hospital immediately. Break speed limits if you have to."

Lois carried Rex to the bathroom, let him empty his bowls, while he puked in a pot. In a few minutes, it drained him from both ends. She put him in a pair of clean pants and a T-shirt. Then she drove him to the hospital.

When they got to the hospital, the doctors were already aware of the situation and started putting cold rags around his neck and forehead. The nurse started an IV and took some samples of blood, urine, bowel, and vomit. They checked his temperature every 15 minutes as it hovered. They determined it was dysentery and asked if Rex had been in or near stagnant water.

Rex said, "We were hunting frogs on Lollipop Lake, and I stepped on a piece of glass. It was bleeding, but I washed it off in the lake water.".

The doctor said, "Oh NO, I know what it is! Get him to a room stat, start him on IV antibiotics, and keep his brain cooled, cold towels on his neck and head! And get a priest!"

He turned to Lois. "He has shigellosis. It's a nasty bacterium that decomposes dead fish and animals in stagnant ponds. If he drank it, he would have a 10% chance of survival. Stepping on the glass put it directly into his bloodstream. The bacteria are trying to decompose his body. If he lives, it will be a miracle. Please wait outside the room and PRAY!"

Entering the room, he was in charge. "We need to work fast if we have any chance of saving him. He's dehydrated. His fever is at 106 and if it hits 107 for longer than 10 minutes, his brain will boil. He could end up mentally retarded even if he lives."

As Rex laid in the bed, stomach cramping in pain, he suddenly felt very calm. The pain had stopped. He looked down and saw the doctors working on him. Then he heard someone call his name. As he moved toward the sound, he saw a long hallway.

His grandmother was there, as well as Uncle Alec and Aunt Lois. But they were dead. How could they be talking to him and smiling at him? They told him to go toward the light. Soon, other dead relatives and friends were lining up. He saw Old Mr. Fields. Rex thought he got killed by his cats. A friend who had died in a car accident. All guided him toward a light.

Suddenly, he was at the end of the hall, and the light blinded him for a moment. He looked and saw a group of men sitting at a table.

One of them stood. "Would you like to stay or go back?"

Rex said, "What would you like me to do, Jesus?"

The man appreciated this answer. "I would like you to go back. You have many important things to do. But you can stay if you don't want to go back."

Rex said, "If I go back, will I come back to heaven again?".

Delighted, he looked at the others as they all smiled. "When the time comes, you will always be welcome back".

Rex said, "If that's what you want, then I will go back."

Suddenly, Rex was screaming. He couldn't see because they covered his head with a diaper soaked in ice cold water. So was the rest of his body. He started thrashing, trying to get the freezing cold diapers off.

The nurse cried out. "Doctor, he's moving. He's ALIVE!"

The doctor looked shocked! "Oh my God, you're back! We thought we'd lost you for a few minutes."

There was a priest standing next to the bed. They put the diaper over his head because they thought Rex was dead.

The priest stepped back, and the doctors started checking vitals. The temperature had dropped to 103. They continued putting on the iced diapers and began a second IV. They put a full syringe of antibiotics into each IV and tried to keep Rex from throwing off the icy blankets.

The doctor went out to Lois. "It was close. We thought we'd lost him for about 2 minutes. It looks like he's going to make it back to the world of the living. It will take several days to get rid of the infection. Now that we know what we're dealing with, we have a good chance of licking it."

Lois cried. "Thank you, God, thank you for another of your miracles."

She had to put on a gown and mask. The infection was not likely to spread, but nobody wanted to take chances.

She held his hand and sang. When Rex fell asleep, she went out into the hall for a cigarette and came back. Rex whimpered, "mom, where have you been?".

Lois said, "I was here just a few minutes ago, don't you remember?"

Rex looked puzzled. "Wasn't that yesterday?"

Time blurred together. Rex seemed to do not know what day or time it was. He had only been in the hospital for a few hours, but it seemed like days. But he couldn't remember anything either.

The doctor worried. "Rex might have suffered brain damage. We'll have to wait and see."

They had to keep Rex in diapers for several days because he got too dehydrated and too tired to use the bedpan. He had lost almost a third of his body weight, and his bones were visible almost everywhere.

Rex drew a self-portrait of himself. One doctor even remarked, "You have big hips, like a girl"

Rex giggled with delight. "Yes! Like a girl!"

The recovery took about 3 weeks. By the time Rex returned to school, the other kids were almost shocked to see how thin he was. He looked almost like a ghost. Rex seemed to be happier, more content. He still didn't want to play with the boys. He stayed close to the teachers or chased grasshoppers in the field.

ALMOST OVER

Rex was still having trouble with math, so he took a special remedial math. It was more like a recipe. He could do smaller bits of multiplication. Then he could put the products together using simpler addition, to get the correct answer. Rex caught up quickly. He liked the math teacher, Mr. Houser, who gave him lots of encouragement.

Rex was reading at college level, writing at high school level. His math skills, especially computational skills, were now at grade level. Rex also loved science and made a beautiful diorama to show ecology. He also loved art, especially perspective drawing.

He put a gouge into his arm when carving leather tiles to make print pads, but they fixed that with a few stitches.

Rex still stayed after school. He tried to play basketball because Mr. Donald was coaching the team and thought that because Rex was so tall, he might be a decent player.

Rex's heart wasn't into it, though. He spent most of the games reading Archie comic books or science magazines. Eventually, he just dropped out. The boys were glad that Rex didn't want to play. He was terrible at basketball.

CRAMPS

Rex continued to get cramps and bleeding stools about once every full moon. It was becoming routine, and Rex could tell when they were about to start and would take a laxative to ease the passing of the plug. The cramps were still incredible, like his insides were being rearranged. However, his parents seemed to take it in stride.

Often, Lois would give him the Darvon or Darvocet to get him through the cramps. The pattern became very predictable, and soon Lois would buy a box of ex-lax when she bought tampons and made sure Rex took them. When Rex asked why, she said "I don't want you keeping me up all night".

Rex tried to push being a girl. He wore slips or his teddy to bed, letting his spaghetti straps show. He hoped that SOMEONE would talk to him about his desire to be a girl. One time, Tom even came in, tucked him in and Rex, still asleep, used his tongue in the kiss. Yet his parents continued to ignore the rhinoceros in the living room.

With Walt and Diane playing down the street all day long, and no desire to do chores, and Lois working full time, Rex found it much easier to spend the entire day dressed as a girl, doing housework, cleaning, vacuuming, making beds, doing laundry, and cooking.

Rex started wearing panties under his pants or shorts that summer. It almost blew up in his face when some older kids wanted to scrub him. Scrubbing was a ritual that all 6th graders went through. It involved being stripped to your undershorts, covered with lipstick, and then taking your pants or shorts. Some kids would keep the scrub on for a few days.

When they approached Rex, he was with his friend Mark. Rex didn't want Mark to know that he dressed like a girl under his pants.

Rex lied. "I'm not a 6th grader, I'm a 5th grader."

It was a close call, and Rex wished he could have gotten it over with so he wouldn't have to worry about it again.

Rex also went on long "bike hikes", often as far as 30 miles each way, pausing only for water, and having a snack on the way back. Rex loved the peace of the back roads, and he loved the way riding his bicycle made his legs so long and smooth.

Sometimes, they would see airplanes flying low, and sometimes even helicopters. One time, he even saw a black helicopter that didn't seem to make any noise at all. As it flew by about a mile from the isolated road, there was no noise at all, until it flew over a hill, when it made the usual rotor noise.

Rex also enjoyed swimming and had reached the point where he could swim 100 meters under water. The breaststroke and side stroke were his favorites. He would often swim for 2-3 hours without a break. Rex tried the high dive, but he spread his legs as he jumped and hurt himself. He enjoyed diving from the low board. Sometimes, he would dive from the low board and swim as far as he could underwater. He got in trouble when he did, and most of the time, he had to come up because he couldn't swim around the crowded shallow part of the pool.

Later that summer, Rex wore the teddy under his pants and t-shirt. One time, he was climbing a tree to a treehouse in another boy's yard when the boy saw the teddy.

He looked at the black chiffon, "what's that"

Rex whimpered, "a teddy".

The boy punched him. "Oh my God, you're a FAIRY! Get out of here!"

Word traveled fast. By the time school started in Jr High, would EVERBODY know?

NUTS!

The summer that Rex was 11. In late August, his testicles came down. Rex panicked. He tried to push them back up inside "where they belong!". If they stayed there, he would become a hairy monster, like a werewolf. His voice would go too low and he'd grew a beard. He would get too tall and too big to wear pretty clothes. He could NEVER be a girl.

Rex devised ways to "destroy the testes". He drew baths of scalding hot water. He would plop down into the water and press his testes into the water to "poach" them, like eggs. Pouring boiling water on them while he was in the tub. Tying them up with Rubber Bands, because he had read that the Australians castrated sheep that way. Using thread and string as well. Even after several weeks, they were still there.

He even tried using a two-by-four and a sledgehammer.

He decided he wouldn't try THAT again.

Several times, when boys would try to kick him between the legs, he would open wide so they could get a clear shot, but they didn't do enough damage.

By age 12, Rex could already see the changes taking place. Instead of singing Soprano in Jr Choir, he had to sing alto because it hurt to sing the high notes. He got taller, growing taller than his mother. This led to a fresh problem. None of her clothes would fit anymore, and he still couldn't buy any.

END BOOK 1

www.ingramcontent.com/pod-product-compliance
Lightning Source LLC
Chambersburg PA
CBHW061236170626
46809CB00007B/2700